Samuel French Acting Edition

This Side of Crazy

by Del Shores

I0589051

ıl SAMUEL FRENCH Iı

Copyright © 2021 by Del Shores
All Rights Reserved

THIS SIDE OF CRAZY is fully protected under the copyright laws of the United States of America, the British Commonwealth, including Canada, and all member countries of the Berne Convention for the Protection of Literary and Artistic Works, the Universal Copyright Convention, and/ or the World Trade Organization conforming to the Agreement on Trade Related Aspects of Intellectual Property Rights. All rights, including professional and amateur stage productions, recitation, lecturing, public reading, motion picture, radio broadcasting, television, online/digital production, and the rights of translation into foreign languages are strictly reserved.

ISBN 978-0-573-70909-8

www.concordtheatricals.com
www.concordtheatricals.co.uk

FOR PRODUCTION INQUIRIES

UNITED STATES AND CANADA
info@concordtheatricals.com
1-866-979-0447

UNITED KINGDOM AND EUROPE
licensing@concordtheatricals.co.uk
020-7054-7200

Each title is subject to availability from Concord Theatricals Corp., depending upon country of performance. Please be aware that *THIS SIDE OF CRAZY* may not be licensed by Concord Theatricals Corp. in your territory. Professional and amateur producers should contact the nearest Concord Theatricals Corp. office or licensing partner to verify availability.

CAUTION: Professional and amateur producers are hereby warned that *THIS SIDE OF CRAZY* is subject to a licensing fee. The purchase, renting, lending or use of this book does not constitute a license to perform this title(s), which license must be obtained from Concord Theatricals Corp. prior to any performance. Performance of this title(s) without a license is a violation of federal law and may subject the producer and/or presenter of such performances to civil penalties. Both amateurs and professionals considering a production are strongly advised to apply to the appropriate agent before starting rehearsals, advertising, or booking a theatre. A licensing fee must be paid whether the title(s) is presented for charity or gain and whether or not admission is charged. Professional/Stock licensing fees are quoted upon application to Concord Theatricals Corp.

This work is published by Samuel French, an imprint of Concord Theatricals Corp.

No one shall make any changes in this title(s) for the purpose of production. No part of this book may be reproduced, stored in a retrieval system, scanned, uploaded, or transmitted in any form, by any means, now known or yet to be invented, including mechanical, electronic, digital, photocopying, recording, videotaping, or otherwise, without the prior written permission of the publisher. No one shall share this title(s), or any part of this title(s), through any social media or file hosting websites.

For all inquiries regarding motion picture, television, online/digital and other media rights, please contact Concord Theatricals Corp.

MUSIC AND THIRD-PARTY MATERIALS USE NOTE

Licensees are solely responsible for obtaining formal written permission from copyright owners to use copyrighted music and/or other copyrighted third-party materials (e.g., artworks, logos) in the performance of this play and are strongly cautioned to do so. If no such permission is obtained by the licensee, then the licensee must use only original music and materials that the licensee owns and controls. Licensees are solely responsible and liable for clearances of all third-party copyrighted materials, including without limitation music, and shall indemnify the copyright owners of the play(s) and their licensing agent, Concord Theatricals Corp., against any costs, expenses, losses and liabilities arising from the use of such copyrighted third-party materials by licensees. For music, please contact the appropriate music licensing authority in your territory for the rights to any incidental music.

IMPORTANT BILLING AND CREDIT REQUIREMENTS

If you have obtained performance rights to this title, please refer to your licensing agreement for important billing and credit requirements.

This is a work of fiction. All the names, characters, businesses, places, events, and incidents in this book are either the product of the author's imagination or used in a fictitious manner. Any resemblance to actual persons, living or dead, or actual events is purely coincidental.

THIS SIDE OF CRAZY was originally commissioned and produced at New Conservatory Theatre Center in San Francisco, California on September 28, 2019 (Artistic Director, Ed Decker; Executive Director, Barbara Hodgen) (Season Producers: Alvin Baum & Robert Holgate, Michael Golden & Michael Levy, Lowell Kimble, Ted Tucker) (Executive Producers: Norman Abramson & David Beery and Charles Matteson & Oakley Stephens) (Producers: Jeff Malloy & Dean Shibuya).

The production was directed by Del Shores, with scenic design by Kate Boyd, technical direction by Carlos Aceves, musical direction by Amy Meyers, wig design by David Carver-Ford, costume design by Wes Crain, prop design by Tom O'Brien, sound design by Kalon Thibodeaux, lighting design by Patrick Toebe, and Jamison Hollister performed/arranged the "City of Gold" track. The stage manager was Emma Gifford, and the assistant stage manager was Emilio Racinez. The original cast, in order of appearance, was as follows:

DITTY . . . . Christine Macomber
RACHEL . . . . Cheryl Smith
BETHANY . . . . Amy Meyers
ABIGAIL . . . . Alison Whismore

THIS SIDE OF CRAZY was produced by Louise H. Beard, Emerson Collins, and Del Shores for Beard Collins Shores Productions at the Zephyr Theatre in Los Angeles, California on January 31, 2020. The play was directed by Del Shores, with scenic design by Tom Buderwitz, costume design by Shon LeBlanc, lighting design by Matthew Brian Denman, and sound design by Drew Dalzell. Musical direction and vocal arrangements were produced by Blake McIver. Jamison Hollister performed and arranged the "City of Gold" track, and additional vocals for songs heard in the play were by Blake McIver, Natali Dorn, and Chelsea Stock. Graphic design was by Sherry Etzel, photography was by Karianne Flaathen, and publicity was by David Elzer. The stage manager was Letitia Chang, and the assistant stage manager was Saige Holst. The cast, in order of appearance, was as follows:

DITTY . . . . Sharon Garrison
RACHEL . . . . Bobbie Eakes
BETHANY . . . . Rachel Sorsa
ABIGAIL . . . . Dale Dickey

Susan Leslie also appeared during the run in the role of Abigail Blaylock.

CHARACTERS

DITTY BLAYLOCK – The matriarch of the family. Seventy, but some "work" has perhaps kept her looking younger. Once a stage mother, she is controlling and narcissistic. Lives for the dramatic and the spotlight.

RACHEL BLAYLOCK – The oldest sister. Forty-eight, pretty, conservative, well-preserved, and can never be wrong.

BETHANY BLAYLOCK – The youngest sister. Forty-five, failed at love over and over, is now an atheist and a lesbian. Most likely has untreated ADHD.

ABIGAIL BLAYLOCK – The middle sister. Forty-six, looks older, beat up by life. Has lots of suppressed anger.

SETTING

The play takes place right outside of Middlesboro, Kentucky at the Blaylock home.

TIME

The play takes place over several days during the fall.

MUSIC NOTE

Lead sheets for "City of Gold" are included at the back of the Acting Edition. This music is intended for both rehearsal and performance of "City of Gold" in Act Two, Scene One. Licensees are also provided with a performance track to be used for the performance of "City of Gold" in Act Two, Scene Four. Both the track and the lead sheets are required for performance.

For
Louise H. Beard

ACT ONE

Scene One

(The set is a cabin-style, two-story home right outside of Middlesboro, Kentucky, nestled in the Smoky Mountains. The home is beyond neat and clean. The family room is the main playing area, with a dining area. The décor is mountain, with a little Laura Ashley thrown in that tells us a woman is in charge here. A stairway leads up to three playing areas: a bedroom with a headboard facing away from the audience; a sun porch where a rocking chair looks out toward the audience, with a day bed beside the chair; and a small landing that separates the entrances to both the bedroom and the porch. A small dresser sits on the landing. Another exit on the landing gives the illusion characters are exiting to more of the house.)

(Day one. Early evening.)

(Family room. Lights are dark as a TV comes on. From the TV, three little girls – ages six, seven, and nine – sing "Farther Along."* Lights stay dark, and only a shadow of a **WOMAN** *lit by the TV can be seen watching the TV and manning the remote. The TV*

---

*A license to produce *This Side of Crazy* does not include a performance license for any third-party or copyrighted recordings. Licensees must create their own, using public domain music.

should be positioned so the audience does not see an image, only hears the audio. More furniture – a coffee table, perhaps another chair or two, and an older, upright piano are also in the room, as well as a small dining table with four chairs.)

(Bedroom. Lights come up slowly on the upstairs bedroom, revealing a moaning **WOMAN** *on top of an unseen man in the bed, hidden by the headboard. Blouse open, revealing a pink bra, the* **WOMAN** *rides the man and enjoys herself as her moans of pleasure get louder. This is* **RACHEL BLAYLOCK HANKS.** *The oldest sister. She's forty-eight, pretty, conservative, and well-preserved. A tube connects the man to a stand with two bags feeding and hydrating him. Other medical indications sitting on the nightstand, such as gauze, medical tape, rubbing alcohol, and peroxide, show us that this man is not well.* **RACHEL** *takes the man's hand and makes the hand feel her breasts as she continues the ride. The man's hand should be fake but look real, or staged in a manner where the man can exit, giving the illusion he is still in the bed throughout the play.)*

(Note: The set may be altered where the porch and bedroom are all on one floor. Perhaps the bedroom stage right off to one side on a riser, with a door connected to the family room and the porch stage left, downstage. Set and furniture are suggestions, but designers are encouraged to be creative to accommodate the theatre with the story being told.)

(Family room. Lights leak upon the **WOMAN** *watching the three little girls. She downs her*

last swig of coffee, puts down the cup, and replaces it with a pistol. She is annoyed by the sounds of Rachel having sex. As an orgasm approaches, she looks toward the bedroom in disgust, points the gun to her head, and pulls the trigger. Click. She puts down the gun, picks up the TV remote, and turns up the volume. As she watches the girls sing on TV, she puts the gun to her head and pulls the trigger another time or two. This is **DOROTHY (DITTY) BLAYLOCK.** *She wears a bright muumuu, a matching turban, is seventy, but some "work" has perhaps kept her looking younger. She's a force to be reckoned with, once a stage mother, has no censor, is a narcissist, lives for the dramatic and the spotlight, and is the most prolific, celebrated songwriter in gospel music history.)*

(Bedroom. During the above, lights also come up more on **RACHEL** *as she has a complete, uncensored orgasm. After her climax, she takes a moment to enjoy the aftermath of feelings, then fixes her bra, buttons her light pink blouse, gets off of the man, and pulls up her panties as her breathing returns to normal. She straightens the bed around the man, checks the bags, then reaches down and kisses him and exits the room, onto:)*

(Landing/family room. **RACHEL** *starts down the stairs, then hears the singing on the TV. She pauses to listen, then descends the stairs, watching the three little girls sing on the TV, then watching* **DITTY** *put the pistol to her head again. Click.)*

RACHEL. Mama, I have told you over and over again, if you are going to play Russian roulette, you need at least one bullet.

DITTY. Oh hush! *(Points to TV as she puts down the pistol.)* Oh Lord, I wish you would look at you and your sisters. Precious, precious, precious. Bring it on home, my little superstars for Jesus!

RACHEL. Another trip down Memory Lane?

DITTY. Yes.

> *(They both watch the TV as the girls finish the song in perfect three-part harmony.* **DITTY** *lowers the volume.)*

RACHEL. Look at how beautiful you were, Mama.

DITTY. Yes –

RACHEL. And that perfect harmony –

DITTY. Yes. Who taught you that, Big Sis?

RACHEL. You did, Mama.

DITTY. Yes –

RACHEL. We were precious. I'll give us that.

> *(***RACHEL*** moves to the couch, sits, starts checking email, etc. on her laptop that sits on the coffee table.)*

DITTY. Yes. Thanks to me. I had those dresses made by that Mexican woman who worked for us when you were little. What was her name?

RACHEL. Maria, Mama. The most common name in the Hispanic culture. And she was Guatemalan.

DITTY. Yes.

RACHEL. Not Mexican.

DITTY. I found those bows on sale down at Sears. Right after Easter. Yellow was Bethany's color, lavender for Abigail and you were always pink. Still are.

(On TV, the crowd claps their enthusiasm. DITTY grabs a tissue and wipes her eyes in order to save her mascara, turns off the TV with her remote, and stores the tissue in her bosom.)

(Sighs.) But then they had to grow up. It is a good thing you did not have children, Rachel. They are disappointments. They *will* disappoint you. One after another. One disappointment right after another. This life is just chocked full of disappointments. And I will be frank with you, most of them are caused by your own children.

RACHEL. Yes mother, I believe we've gone over this a few hundred times.

DITTY. Some things need to be repeated. Helps me cope.

RACHEL. Thus the need to play Russian roulette with an empty gun on a daily basis. Are you done with this nonsense?

*(**RACHEL** gets up, takes the gun, and stores it in a drawer in a cabinet by the front door, then returns to the couch.)*

DITTY. For now, yes. And I do not do that daily. Three, four times a week. Tops. It calms me. Helps me cope. Helps me know there's a nearby exit if I need one. Gives me a sense that I'm in control. And someday, I just might add a bullet – or six. Especially on days when I can hear my eldest daughter having carnal relations with a man in a coma!

RACHEL. You are such a liar! You did not hear –!

DITTY. The heck I didn't. It's a good thing our closest neighbor is two miles up the road – and elderly!

RACHEL. Well, I guess I lost control again. I have absolutely no memory of making any sound.

DITTY. Well, I sure do! Vivid memories! And they are not memories that I cherish!

RACHEL. *(Embarrassed.)* Okay, okay, sorry. I'll be...quieter. *(Re: computer, excited.)* Oh! My latest episode of "Good Christian Women" is already over 26,000 views in only six days.

DITTY. *(Sarcastic.)* Woo, woo. What's this one about?

RACHEL. It's called "A Good Christian Woman's Modern Place In A Marriage."

DITTY. Hmmm. Did you cover a modern place for good Christian women having carnal relations with a husband in a coma?

> (DITTY *gets tickled.* RACHEL *glares at her.* DITTY *tries to compose herself.)*

I'm sorry. I should have just thought that. You know at my age I've started saying whatever pops in this old brain of mine.

RACHEL. Started?! You're just not capable Mama. You've never been. You've always just said whatever you wanted with no regard for who you are hurting. Even when we were little girls. No wonder you only have a relationship with one out of three daughters! And that one is getting more precarious by the day.

DITTY. *(Tearing up.)* That was mean, Rachel. Uncalled for, spiteful and mean.

RACHEL. Well, I learned from the master! *(Shakes her head.)* "One disappointment right after another."

DITTY. Well, *you* were certainly the *least* of my disappointments.

RACHEL. How do you not know that is *not* a compliment?!

DITTY. Well, this I do know. I was a good mother. *(False emotion. Or is it?)* Your daddy turned his back on

Jesus, left his beautiful wife and his precious, precious, precious daughters for that...that harlot and didn't have another thing to do with us. *(Drops emotion, angrily.)* God, I just hope he's lived a miserable, unhappy life! I do. And I hope his ding-dong stopped working and he got one of those sexually transmitted diseases that causes warts!

RACHEL. *(Laughing.)* Mama –

DITTY. I do! I know that's unChristian, but so be it. So, what did your mean mama do? I survived. We survived. And in style, Big Sis. In style! I took my talent...with your talents and made you little superstars for Jesus. Now, I may have made mistakes –

RACHEL. May have? Let's get this straight. You made mistakes, Mama! You made mistakes!

DITTY. Okay! But I did the best I could with the hand I was dealt! I was a good mother. Not a perfect mother, but a good one. And I sleep like a baby at night.

RACHEL. Yeah, with pills.

DITTY. Sometimes I don't like you.

RACHEL. Well, we're even.

DITTY. Who else, I ask you...who else do you know who has been on "The Johnny Carson Show" –

RACHEL. It was called "The Tonight Show" –

DITTY. Well, who else do you know who has been on "The Tonight Show"... *(Yelling.)* STARRING JOHNNY CARSON? The "Merv Griffin Show," "Phil Donahue" and "Sally Jessy Raphael"? Who under the age of ten do you know who has had the opportunity that you and your sisters were given? Huh? Who? Won a Grammy as a teenager? Do you really think anybody would give a rat's patootie about your "Good Christian Woman" thingie thang on that internet nonsense if it hadn't been for me and my efforts that created the Blaylock

Sisters?! Look at this house! It's all yours when I'm gone. We lived the high life. High on the hog. Why? Because of your mean, horrible mama, Rachel!

RACHEL. Okay, okay! Let's just stop. How many times –? Huh? Let's just have some supper. Eat supper, watch the news and go to bed. I'm sorry. You did...great... Mama.

DITTY. *(Tearing up.)* Okay. Okay. Thank you. That means so much, Big Sis. Oh Rachel, y'all were such precious little girls. No wonder America fell in love with you. And there were good times. Your childhood was not a nightmare like you have said so often – which hurts my feelings to the core of my soul and perhaps caused that mild heart attack, not fried food. Stress is worse than fried food. Dr. Oz says that's a medical fact. And right now... *(Crying, or is she?)* My heart hurts. Words cannot be taken back –

RACHEL. Exactly, Mama –

DITTY. But I was a good mama. Don't you remember the good times, Rachel? Name one good time –

RACHEL. I'm not playing this –!

DITTY. Just one good memory for your mama. Please.

RACHEL. *(Sighs.)* Okay, yes... There were good times. Until there weren't. And sometimes well...I think we all felt – *(Stops.)* Why have you started rehashing things we stopped talking about years ago? And why in heavens have you been dragging out all those old videos lately and watching us way back when?

> (**RACHEL** *gets up and starts cleaning the already clean house. She puts up the video that's in the machine, picks up the stack of other videos, orders them, takes a tissue from the coffee table, and dusts.)*

DITTY. Felt what? You all felt what? I need to know what you felt, Rachel. You didn't finish that particular sentence.

RACHEL. *(Pause.)* Felt trapped! It was a lot of pressure, Mama. I think all the pressure...well, maybe that's what caused Abigail to snap, why Bethany went off and did all that...that scandalous stuff.

DITTY. Yes, one daughter put away for attempted murder and one doesn't even believe in God. And you wonder why I get that gun out? But Abigail snapped because of *you*, Big Sis. Your actions caused that whole ordeal that changed *everything*...for all of us.

RACHEL. Stop! Just stop it! Why are you living in the past lately?

DITTY. Because that's what old people do!

RACHEL. *(Laughs.)* Okay, okay. *(Takes her mother in.)* You and me...I think we're more alike than either one of us would like to admit.

DITTY. Two peas in a pod. That's what Aunt Renzie always said about us. Although she's crazy as an outhouse rat. *(Long pause, turns and looks out the window. Distant.)* Can you point to the day you stopped being happy, Rachel? *(Tears up.)* Because I can.

RACHEL. Mama, please! Why do you need to –?

DITTY. Because I need to sort things out, Rachel. So I can make good on a promise I made.

RACHEL. What on earth are you talking about?

DITTY. *(Stares at a picture of the three little girls.)* I want them to come home.

RACHEL. What?

DITTY. I want to get Abigail out, and I wrote Bethany and want her to come back for a visit. My girls together again in the same home where they grew up. Try and reclaim the happy times.

RACHEL. Mama, are you dying? Is there something I don't know? Do you have cancer?

DITTY. Yes. No! I don't have cancer, but...I have stopped being happy. I stopped the day I drove away from that place where I had to put Abigail and realized that life... life was over the way we knew it. Bethany hightailed it out of here and you and me...just us...the last of the Mohicans were left...and I had no real purpose anymore.

RACHEL. Oh, Mama, you do –

DITTY. No, I don't, Rachel. But yes, there is something I need to tell you. Sit down.

RACHEL. Oh no. No no no. I do not like sit-downs.

DITTY. *(Losing it.)* I need you to sit down! I need you to sit down!! I need you to sit down!!!

> (**DITTY** *points to a chair at the dining room table.* **RACHEL** *glares at* **DITTY**, *goes to the dining room table, and sits.* **DITTY** *joins her.)*

(Sweetly.) Thank you. *(Proud.)* I, Ditty Blaylock... I am being honored by GMT – Gospel Music Television is honoring your mama, Ditty Blaylock! There's gonna be a big special with stars far and wide singing all the songs I've written in tribute to me and telling stories about me. Lord, I hope they're kind. Amy Grant and Vince Gill, Carrie Underwood, Dolly, Sandi Patty is trying to get out of a prior engagement in Dallas... Steven Curtis Chapman...Michael W. Smith...even Shirley Caesar has forgiven me for that comment I made that was misconstrued as racist and she is coming – and that's just the start of the list. The living legend, Ditty Blaylock...their words, not mine...fifty

years of singing and writing songs for Jesus. Creator and mother of the Blaylock Sisters...your very own mama is being honored.

RACHEL. Well that's wonderful, Mama. Congratulations. I'll help you shop for the perfect outfit. When did you get the news?

DITTY. About a month ago no...three weeks and two days ago.

RACHEL. And you're just telling me this now?

DITTY. Yes. Because...I wanted to...well, try and figure out how to do this without your help –

RACHEL. Do what?!

DITTY. Well, there's something else...a hitch...a serious problem. A little hiccup. I promised them something. *(Nervous, rapidly spewing it out.)* I made a promise to the producer – Tucker Davis – and he now expects the Blaylock Sisters. He said, "Well, your special would be extra special if we could get the Blaylock Sisters back together. The ratings would be through the roof." And without thinking, I said, "Oh, that's easy! Done deal." I said it without really thinking it through, but now I have and... *(Accelerates nervous rant.)* Rachel, he's more excited about y'all reuniting than about Carrie Underwood saying yes. She's going to talk about how she grew up on my music in Oklahoma, how when she accepted Jesus, the night she walked down the aisle, the special music was a Ditty Blaylock song... I can't remember which one, but it's a beautiful, heartfelt story which she shared on "American Idol" but they edited out. You know how the Jews run Hollywood. Tucker is trying to get that footage. And the girls can stay here for a few days, rehearse...figure out what to sing...and y'all can be sisters again. Oh, Rachel, I want to find us some happy times again and create some new, good memories like we saw tonight on the TV when you were singing, little superstars for Jesus. Be a family before I go to meet my maker, so I can die in peace, completed. This is all I have left to offer this world, then ol' Ditty Blaylock is done! I can die in peace. Happy. Knowing my daughters have each other again. My little superstars for Jesus will reunite, one last time. That's what I promised. Is that too much to ask for?

(**RACHEL** *just stares, then gets up and heads to the kitchen.*)

RACHEL. Yes!

(*Blackout.*)

Scene Two

(Day two. Morning.)

*(Family room. Lights up on **DITTY** as she enters from the kitchen, carrying a cup of coffee, humming and singing "City of Gold," wearing another bright muumuu, same turban. She picks up a box of stationary on the credenza, sits at the table, and starts looking through some envelopes she has addressed.)*

DITTY. *(Mumbling.)* Let's see. Amy and Vince. Carrie. *(Smiles.)* Dolly. *(With judgment.)* Shirley Caesar. Sandi – *(Suddenly remembering something.)* Oh!

*(She puts the envelopes aside, grabs another piece of stationary, and starts writing. **RACHEL**, dressed casually for the day, enters the landing from the "hall" entrance, glances down the stairs, then goes into the bedroom. She checks the levels on Jude's bags, kisses him, then exits and descends the stairs.)*

RACHEL. *(Terse.)* Morning.

DITTY. *(Overly sweet.)* Morning, my sweet oldest daughter who I love from the depths of my heart and soul.

RACHEL. *(Long pause, just staring.)* Sleep well?

DITTY. Yes – *(Sarcastic.)* With pills. Because I've led such a horrible life that I wouldn't be able to get a wink of sleep otherwise.

RACHEL. *(Another long pause, staring.)* Who are you writing?

DITTY. The girls. I haven't heard back from them. I just want to get Abigail out and back home – not forever, just for a week of rehearsal and the show – then I'll take her back to the facility.

RACHEL. Okay, we have to talk –

DITTY. *(Forging on.)* She likes it there, you know? Well, how would you know? You've never gone to see her once. Probably wouldn't recognize her if you ran into her on the street. For the best. That she's there. Beats prison where all those lesbian convicts rape you. And I'd love to see if we can get Bethany on the right track, back with the Lord, singing for Jesus. Wouldn't that just be glorious? A good taste of Jesus and family and I bet she'll be back on the straight and narrow. This could be her gospel comeback. You both could go solo! Or form a new duo.

RACHEL. An atheist gospel singer. What a wonderful idea.

DITTY. Oh, she's not a real atheist. Nobody is really an atheist. Imagine the press she'd get if she repented for her wicked, wicked ways and made a comeback. Bethany, of course, always was the best singer. Not the prettiest...you were always that...but certainly the best singer.

RACHEL. Yes, Mama, you've pointed that out since we were children.

> *(**RACHEL** settles on the couch, opens her computer, and checks her social media and email.)*

DITTY. Kids need to know the truth. I sent them both sweet letters a week ago on this precious stationary you gave me for Mother's Day. *(Waves it.)* At the time, I thought it was a useless gift, a Walmart afterthought, but it was perfect for writing and asking my girls, my precious daughters. *(Pointedly.)* To remind them of the good times. And I offered to pay them. Sent them unsigned checks for five thousand dollars each. How clever was that? They have to come here in order for me to sign them! And I will be glad to pay you as well. I don't have to pay Abigail or even ask her if she'll do this...bein's I have guardianship...but, woo, she's so headstrong, best to make her think she's in on the decision. If she's mad, can't make that one sing. Must I remind you of that fiasco in Shreveport. I have never been so humiliated. When you stole her lavender bow and she refused to perform?

RACHEL. You are unbelievable! Aren't you forgetting something?

DITTY. Honey, I'm past seventy. I'm sure I am. Pray tell, what am I forgetting?

RACHEL. The promise you made to me? That if I allowed you to cover up what she did that she'd stay locked up and away from me – and Jude! Forever!

DITTY. I'm not breaking that promise! She will continue to be locked up. After my special.

RACHEL. THAT WAS NOT PART OF THE PROMISE!

DITTY. Well, how was I to know that I would be bestowed such an honor with these conditions!

RACHEL. YOU MADE THESE CONDITIONS! And what makes you think I'll be part of this reunion? You're just making an assumption! You can't make me sing either! And I don't need your money!

DITTY. Rachel, darlin', sugar plum dumplin', would you deny your poor mama –

RACHEL. Yes!

DITTY. Oh! I nearly forgot. Tucker Davis sent me an email just last night and Larry Gatlin has also asked to perform. Tucker thinks that ship has sailed and docked, but I think we should let him in, don't you? Said my music got him through rehab –

RACHEL. I. Don't. Care! I have to tape my new segment. Maybe this episode should be on how *not* to kill your manipulative mother when you're at your rope's end –

DITTY. I am not manipulative!

RACHEL. Ha! Manipulative *and* delusional!

DITTY. Okay, fine! I'll just call it off! *(Rises, rushes around the room.)* I'll call Tucker Davis right now and tell him to cancel the show because I cannot deliver the Blaylock Sisters! Fine! Fine! Have it your way, Rachel! I am so tired. I feel like I've been sent for but I'm too tired to go! I'm just so tired of life...and you...and now I have nothing left to live for! And you are *not* honoring your mother, like the Bible says to do! So, no, I'm not even going to play Russian roulette this time, I am simply going to put a gun to my head and kill myself. I'm not even going to make a fun, little game out of my suicide. Where's the telephone? *(Looks for it.)* Where'd you leave the telephone? Let me call Tucker Davis first, and I'm gonna tell him to hold the presses, that the show is over, not going to happen! Finito! Alert the stars to NOT save the date! Go ahead and book a county fair in Amarillo or in...in Boone County...or book that pot-infested, drug festival hippy thing that Willie Nelson has every year in Texas. Book something else, stars, because "The Ditty Blaylock Fifty-Years Of Serving Jesus Special" is *not* going to happen. It's off! Canceled! I'm not going to tell him that my own daughters will not reunite for me...no I will not tell him that...because that will make me look bad. And y'all will look like the ungrateful little bitches that you are. Yes, that's what I said! BITCHES! It will make me look as if I am unloved by my own daughters, which is true, but the public should never know that. I won't let them know that my oldest daughter Rachel would not put things aside so –

RACHEL. Put things aside?! Well, I'm sorry, but it's really hard to put aside attempted murder, Mama, that left my husband in a coma for almost twenty-five years!

DITTY. *(As she tears up the notes.)* Sorry Shirley! Not gonna happen. Sorry Carrie, Vince and Amy. Sandi, do not even think of canceling that engagement in Dallas! It'll be much easier to call Tucker Davis, who will be devastated and cancel the whole event and then kill myself. Save Larry Gatlin the humiliation of being turned down. Will probably send him right back to drugs and pillin'. Let's take the easy way out, shall we?

> (**DITTY** *throws all the torn-up letters in the air, scattering them on the floor.* **RACHEL** *finds the phone and puts in on the table in front of* **DITTY**. *She then goes and grabs the gun, a package of bullets, and slams them on the table.*)

RACHEL. You're all set! Do it Mama! Just do it! But please go out to your thinking and songwriting spot by the creek when you shoot yourself because I do not need another mess in this house to clean up!!! *(Picking up Ditty's torn-up letters.)* Next flood, the blood will all be washed away! Spare me that if you don't mind. And hurry up because I need to film my episode of "GOOD CHRISTIAN WOMEN"!

> (**RACHEL** *storms up the stairs.* **DITTY** *stares after her and sighs, defeated. Doorbell.*)

DITTY. Well, who in the world? Coming!

> (**DITTY** *answers the door, revealing* **BETHANY BLAYLOCK**, *the youngest sister. A very hot, hard-bodied forty-five. She has failed at marriage and love too many times to count, is now an atheist and a lesbian, and is always thinking, questioning, and most likely has untreated ADHD.* **BETHANY** *wears jeans and a revealing, yellow tank top, carries a suitcase in one hand, and holds a check in the other.*)

BETHANY. Well...I made it. Hello, Mama.

DITTY. Bethany! Lil' Sis! Come love my neck!

(They hug, then **BETHANY** *hands* **DITTY** *the check.)*

BETHANY. Sign this...please.

(Blackout.)

Scene Three

(Day three. Around noon.)

(Family room. Lights up on **RACHEL** *dressed in a pink, dressy ensemble, holding her white Bible. She sits in a chair and begins recording her episode of "Good Christian Women" on an iPhone that is positioned on a tripod in front of her. There is an obvious difference in her TV persona, which is upbeat and saccharine, with a touch of false sincerity but real emotion.)*

RACHEL. My good Christian women. Proverbs 21:23 teaches: *(Reading from her white Bible.)* "He who guards his mouth and his tongue guards his soul from troubles." Well my my my. A mighty tall order to fill sometimes, isn't it? Now let's go back a few chapters to Proverbs 15:1. *(Reads.)* "A gentle answer turns away wrath, but a harsh word stirs up anger." Um, um, um. Ladies, my warrior sisters in Christ, that scripture speaks so loud to me today. Let me ask you a question. How many love your family? Your mama, your daddy, your sisters, brothers, cousins, uncles, aunts...well, you get it...and yet, you don't always *like* Brother Tommy or Aunt Sally or Sister Margaret or even your very own mama?! What do you do about that? Well this is not Biblical, but I say: Choose. Your. Battles. Some battles are simply just not worth fighting. Some battles are not worthy of fighting. Not worthy of *you*. And sometimes, yes, sometimes, you have to swallow your pride. You have to just hold your tongue simply to keep peace. And yes, we love our mamas and our daddies, our siblings... but we have to realize...and this is not biblical...this is something I heard long ago. Are you ready? 'Cause this is a doozy, might just knock you right off your feet. They push your buttons *because they installed them.* Let that sink in, would ya? And sometimes we have to practice forgiveness no matter what the crime is. And yes, sisters, I'm preaching to myself. *(Chokes up.)* I, Rachel Blaylock Hanks, am a human being just like you…and I am a sinner just like you…and sometimes I say things and do things that I regret and are not pure of heart that I wish I could take back. So, y'all… think, pray and don't forget to love your families and love Jesus. I am Rachel Blaylock Hanks. I strive daily to be a good Christian woman. Join me on this quest, my warrior sisters in Christ. Until we meet again.

> *(RACHEL blows a kiss to the camera, turns the iPhone off, drops the TV persona, gets up, returns the tripod to its storage place, then heads up the stairs and enters Jude's room.)*

> *(Bedroom. RACHEL takes a deep breath, goes and checks the hanging bags, adjusts Jude, and straightens his covers.)*

Hey baby… *(Starts to cry.)* I am about to come unglued.

> *(A car sputters up in front of the house.)*

I feel like my person is about to come out of my skin and just explode into the air into a hundred million pieces.

> *(Family room. The door opens and BETHANY walks in, wearing the same jeans, another tank top. She carries an envelope while juggling two bags of groceries in Dollar General bags. She walks over to the dining table, places the bags on it, takes out a wad of cash from the envelope, and shakes her head in amazement.)*

(Calling.) Bethany…that you? Bethany?

BETHANY. *(Calling.)* Yes. I'm back. Check was good. Got my money.

(**RACHEL** *exits the bedroom, talks to* **BETHANY** *from the stairs.*)

RACHEL. Come on up. Come see Jude.

BETHANY. Oh... I think... I don't know... If I'm ready... You know, to see him.

RACHEL. Okay. But I wish you would. (*Gets emotional.*) I don't really have anybody to talk to about all this... Except him... And he doesn't say much. (*Off* **BETHANY***'s confused look.*) That's a little coma humor. It's okay to laugh.

(**BETHANY** *returns the money to the envelope, sets it on the table.*)

BETHANY. I see. Okay, I'll come... I'll come up there.

RACHEL. Thank you.

(**RACHEL** *leads* **BETHANY** *up the stairs and into the bedroom.* **BETHANY** *hesitates by the doorway, taking Jude in.*)

Remember Jude? Jude, Bethany's here to visit you.

BETHANY. Can he hear?

RACHEL. I don't know...the doctor says probably...but...I tried to teach him to squeeze my hand once for yes and twice for no like they told me to, but...nothing. They said his brain is mostly gray matter.

BETHANY. Gray matter. That sounds just awful. Gray is such an ugly color. Oh my God! I read in this magazine there was this guy in Canada who had a stroke and the only muscle that could work was his sphincter...and he could say yes or no by squeezing once or twice.

RACHEL. I have so many questions that I'm not willing to ask!

BETHANY. Mama told me...well, that he...that Jude is capable of, you know –

RACHEL. Sex?

BETHANY. Yes. I believe her exact words were... *(Imitating Ditty.)* "They have carnal relations, Baby Sis. It's just sick, sick, sick."

(They share a laugh.)

RACHEL. Well, he is my husband. And we both enjoy it. I mean, he certainly seems to enjoy it judging from his –

*(As **BETHANY** listens intently, **RACHEL** stops abruptly, realizing she's oversharing. **RACHEL** takes in **BETHANY**, settling on her ample cleavage.)*

So...are you still...stripping?

BETHANY. *(Pause.)* No...I'm not. I got too old. Stripping is not as easy as it looks, and it's very hard on relationships.

RACHEL. Oh! You're in a relationship –?

BETHANY. Yes. Well no. It's very complicated.

RACHEL. Well, I'm just glad you quit...stripping. Nobody wants their baby sister stripping for strange men.

BETHANY. *(Defensive.)* It was a job, okay? And I'm going to miss some of it...you know, my regulars...politicians, businessmen, mostly married. Even a deacon at First Baptist Church of Nashville. I called him Brother Jack. He was so funny...always came in wearing a fishing hat with lures on it...and sunglasses, thought he was in disguise. Would head straight for a private booth and I'd meet him there... I'd make him take off that hat, didn't need a fishing hook hookin' me in the eye... I'd grind and gyrate and walk away with at least a hundred. But then, Brother Jack found someone new...they all do...there was always fresh meat coming in...younger fresh meat... And bam! Self-esteem was...shot again. Fat little Bethany would emerge. What did Mama used to say, "You're not fat, Bethany, you're just fleshy? You'll grow out of it."

RACHEL. Well, she was right...for once. You did grow out of it. You look amazing. You should not be suffering from low self-esteem.

BETHANY. Thank you. Pole dancing and running has kept this old body thin. I still run like six miles a day. Sometimes when I'm runnin' I think...who are you running from? Then I remember. Oh, her! I'm running from Ditty Blaylock! And from that big bad, mean vengeful God we were all taught to fear. Okay...there's something else...that I'm scared to tell you.

RACHEL. Try me. I can't imagine anything being worse than you being a stripper who is also an atheist. *(Pause.)* What?

BETHANY. *(Nervous, deep breath.)* I'm...a lesbian.

> (**RACHEL** *is silent, stares, stunned.* **BETHANY** *nods.*)

(Slowly.) I am a lesbian –

RACHEL. Yes. I heard you! Oh dear Lord! You can't tell Mama. It would be...it would be just too much for her to handle. That's one thing she can die not knowing. You stripping almost sent her to an early grave. There's just always something...new with you.

BETHANY. *(To Jude.)* She says with judgment.

> (**RACHEL** *sighs and shakes her head as* **BETHANY** *stares at Jude for a long moment.*)

He's so skinny...gaunt...old...he got so old. *(Softly.)* Gray is such an ugly color. He was truly one of the most beautiful men that God ever put on this earth. *(Laughs.)* I'm an atheist and I just alluded that there is a God, and I'm a lesbian and kinda lusting after your husband...not this Jude, but Jude back then.

RACHEL. I think you really do believe in God.

BETHANY. *(Distant.)* I found it was easier to not believe in God than to stay mad at him all the time. *(Stares at Jude.)* You wanna know the saddest thing to me about all of this... About Jude just laying there day after day... what is it...twenty-five years ago?

RACHEL. Twenty-four years, four months...seventeen days.

BETHANY. What's saddest to me about this whole thing – *(Picks up Jude's hand.)* These hands. Nobody could play piano like Jude. He was like a brother to all of us. A big brother. Until...he and Abigail fell in love... And then you had to fall in love with him, too...and steal your sister's fiancé. You never lost at anything, Big Sis.

RACHEL. We can't be blamed for feelings, can we? And love.

BETHANY. No. We can't.

> *(BETHANY exits, upset. RACHEL follows, closes the door. Lights dim in the bedroom and come up in the family room as they walk down the stairs.)*

RACHEL. *(Defensive.)* And I did lose at something. I lost him. She took him away. And as angry as you are at God, well...I'm just as angry at Abigail! What she did was unforgivable!

BETHANY. Okay, okay. I'm sorry... I need to be more... empathetic.

> *(RACHEL goes to the couch, opens her computer, and checks her email.)*

That's what my shrink used to tell me. Dr. Welton. You know, the one who Mama would pay for. But, I had to stop going. Mama stopped paying when I started stripping...or when I slipped and finally told her. Why on earth I told her is beyond me. She cut me off and our royalties had dwindled down to practically nothing.

(**RACHEL** *looks away, knows something.*)

So, I decided to stay *screwed* up...to spite her. And I started thinking...can we really be fixed? *(Doesn't wait for an answer.)* But, I do try and remember to be empathetic. But you know, I always see the word "pathetic" in the word empathetic. Why do you think they put that word in that word?

RACHEL. I have no idea. My God, your mind...it hasn't changed.

BETHANY. *(Softly.)* No, always thinking. Too much. My mind just hops around like the Easter Bunny. Just this side of crazy. And I'm never sure what side I'm on. *(Goes to the table, picks up the envelope full of cash, looks at it.)* Maybe I flip-flop from one side to another. My mind is like a bad neighborhood. You don't want to go there alone.

RACHEL. So...is it just the money... Is that why you came back? Just for the money?

BETHANY. I needed... I've missed my family. Even Mama... bizarre, yes, but I wanted to see that old battle-axe who pushes *all* my buttons.

RACHEL. Because she installed them!

(**RACHEL** *closes the computer as* **BETHANY** *is in and out of the kitchen.*)

BETHANY. Oh that's good! Did you make that up right here on the spot?

(**BETHANY** *takes a bag to the kitchen.*)

RACHEL. *(Calling.)* No, Oprah... I think Oprah said it to Wynonna Judd about Naomi.

BETHANY. *(Returning.)* Oh, I miss Oprah! And the Judds!

(**BETHANY** *pulls out a can of chili from the other bag, shows* **RACHEL.**)

I thought I'd make chili. Shock Mama to show her I learned to cook. Well, sorta. I was so excited when I saw that Dollar General. When they put that in? I'm obsessed with this off-brand of chili...Cooks Chili. *(Shows items.)* It's so good when you add hamburger meat and an onion and garlic salt. I can get about eight to ten meals out of four cans of this chili when I add the other sh...stuff to it. *(Exiting.)* Who needs vegetables!

RACHEL. *(Calling after her.)* You got hamburger meat at the Dollar General? Was it a dollar? I didn't know they sold meat there. Onions are vegetables.

BETHANY. *(Calling from offstage.)* Oh, right, they sure are. Yeah, they sell it. They sell everything...mostly for a dollar. Thus the name of the store.

RACHEL. I worry about you buying meat for a dollar.

(**BETHANY** *returns with a Diet Coke and settles at the table.* **RACHEL** *joins her.*)

BETHANY. *(Laughing.)* We used to eat Vienna sausages right out of the can when we were little. And poor. Before we made our first record. On those car tours before we got the bus. And we LOVED Vienna sausages. The three of us would share one can and get two sausages each, remember? God knows what the ingredients are in Vienna sausages.

RACHEL. We didn't know any better! Now we do. *(Long pause.)* Why did you leave just right after –? Jude was gone and then you...you just left during all the chaos. I needed you. Needed...someone besides Mama who was orchestrating the biggest cover-up in the history of Kentucky.

BETHANY. It sounded so ludicrous when she sat us down and told us what she had done and instructed us what we had to do. But sometimes when I'm mad at Mama, I think...that was love, what she did for Abigail. Preventing her from going to prison.

RACHEL. Ha! Are you kidding! That was *not* love! That was a desperate act to save face! She did it to save herself – and us – from public humiliation! She did it to save her name! Ditty Blaylock cannot have a daughter convicted of attempted murder! And yes...it was ludicrous...blaming it on... *(Imitating* **DITTY.***)* "a wetback who strangled Jude for his pocket watch and ran back across the border to Mexico never to be seen or heard of again." *(Pause, thinks, almost distant.)* Oh Bethany, it was truly the hardest period of my life. I lost you and Jude...and her...all at the same time. You left! You just up and left. Barely even said goodbye. All I was left with was Ditty Blaylock.

BETHANY. *(Sighs.)* I wanted out. And I saw an exit. I knew with all the chaos...the cover-up...the Blaylock Sisters were over...and I just wanted... I needed out. I just wasn't capable. I wanted out. I felt like...I think...well, like Jude. Just trapped. Trapped inside this house...the group...Mama. Mama! Weren't you exhausted? Mama just drained every ounce of...everything...right from us. Just milked us dry. I didn't know who I was. So, I fled. I didn't know what I wanted. But I knew what I didn't want. So, I fled to Nashville thinking I was gonna be the next Reba or Dolly or Miranda. But I soon found out...without the Blaylock Sisters... *(Almost a whisper.)* I was a...nobody.

> *(The door opens and* **DITTY** *enters, wearing an eventful wig and bright pantsuit.)*

DITTY. *(Announcing.)* The Blaylock Sisters are together again!

(**DITTY** *turns to the door, arm stretched out in a presenting fashion as* **ABIGAIL** *tentatively enters. She is the middle sister. She's forty-six but looks older and has lots of suppressed anger. She is wearing an older, dated dress and carrying a beat-up, once-green suitcase. She looks around the house and her eyes glisten over.* **RACHEL** *and* **BETHANY** *just stare, then* **RACHEL**'s *face turns to rage. She grabs her purse from the coffee table.*)

DITTY. Rachel –?

(**RACHEL** *storms past* **DITTY** *and* **ABIGAIL** *and exits.*)

(*Blackout.*)

Scene Four

(Day three. Dusk.)

(Porch. Dim lights up on **ABIGAIL** *sitting, rocking, smoking, staring, wearing a very worn lavender robe.)*

(Family room. Lights up on **DITTY** *staring out the front door.)*

DITTY. *(Calling.)* Bethany! Lil' Sis! Why on earth are you just running around the property over and over?

BETHANY. *(Offstage.)* Running from you, Mama. *(Laughs.)*

DITTY. Oh, you silly-nilly. As feeble as I am these days, I'll sure never catch you. Any sign of Big Sis?

BETHANY. *(Offstage.)* No ma'am.

DITTY. Look down the road towards town. She's been gone for hours. I'm starting to worry.

BETHANY. *(Offstage.)* Still nothing.

DITTY. Well, you better wrap up that...that running nonsense. It's nearly dark. The Boogeyman is lurking behind those trees over there, just waiting for darkness to snatch up pretty little girls.

(No answer. **DITTY** *closes the door.)*

(Mutters.) Exercise is so silly.

(She starts to walk up the stairs.)

(Calling.) Abigail!!! You alright?

ABIGAIL. *(Calling.)* Yes, ma'am. Just watching the sunset.

*(**DITTY** then remembers something, checks her wristwatch, rushes over to the table, grabs a bottle of pills, shakes them, then walks up the*

stairs. On the landing, she opens a drawer in the dresser, pulls out some sheets and a blanket, then opens the door to the porch to find **ABIGAIL** *sitting and smoking. She waves the air to register her disgust, which* **ABIGAIL** *ignores.* **DITTY** *sets the sheets and blanket on the daybed, then sits on it during:)*

DITTY. Hello, Midl' Sis. Are you sure you want to sleep out here on the sun porch? You are welcome to share my big ol' king-size bed, just like when you were a little bitty thang and used to get scared when thunder sounded and lightning would strike, lighting up the whole house for a flash...which it does so often here in Kentucky...in the summertime.

ABIGAIL. I like it out here. The fresh air. At Meadowbrook, they lock us up tighter than a drum at night...gets stuffy... I miss the night fresh air. Look at the sunset, Mama.

DITTY. Yes. Spectacular. I wrote about the sunset more than once.

> *(Singing.)*

WHERE THE SUN NEVER SETS AND THE LEAVES NEVER FALL...

WHERE THE RIGHTEOUS FOREVER WILL SHINE LIKE THE STARS.

Oh! That's the one song that resonates with me most these days as my own sun is slowly setting. The Blaylock Sisters' first big hit.

ABIGAIL. Brings back many memories, that's for sure.

> **(DITTY** *watches* **ABIGAIL** *ash her cigarette on the floor.)*

DITTY. Yes. *(Points.)* Here's some bed things for you.

(**DITTY** *goes and picks up the tray of a small terracotta pot and hands it to* **ABIGAIL** *to use as an ashtray.*)

There's more blankets in the hall if you get cold. Gets chilly out here at night. (*Distant, sad, looking at the sunset.*) I don't write songs anymore. Oh, an idea hits me every now and again, but they just don't roll out of me like they once did. Maybe I've run outta rhymes and said all I need to say.

(**DITTY** *sighs, lost in thought for a moment, fixed on the sunset, then makes the daybed for* **ABIGAIL.**)

I'll get you a pillow from my bed and bring it in. I have real nice down ones I got on sale...somewhere...don't remember where. Had a coupon. Soft, but not too flat. I like a little volume in my pillow.

ABIGAIL. Thank you.

DITTY. (*Hugs* **ABIGAIL.**) It's good to have you home, Midl' Sis. I'm sorry about your room.

(**DITTY** *grabs a broom and sweeps the ashes, then some of the porch, then settles back on the daybed.*)

Turned it into a display of awards and show posters and career such and all. I try to keep a home a home and not a museum for my career, so devoting one room seemed right. You can't believe the paperwork I still have to do...and fan mail. Lord, it just never stops. Not that I want it to. That's when you know you're done, when the fan mail stops. Nail the coffin closed when the fan mail stops. The Blaylock Sisters even get fan mail. Not as much as I do, but enough to matter. You still have fans, Abigail. People you've touched...lives, broken hearts and broken lives, that you help put back together with our music. There was this one girl who wrote me from Kansas...or was it Missouri? Midwest somewhere. Maybe Nebraska. Anyway, told me that her mama got pancreatic cancer...that's what got Dalinda Baker...'member Dalinda? Death sentence... and painful...ooh-wee, I do not want to die in pain, lingering like Dalinda did. Just shoot me like an old show pony with a broken leg when I get too feeble to enjoy life. So...anyway...that girl who wrote me, whose mama had pancreatic cancer...she played her our music every day...our music played for her sweet, dying mama until the very moment she went on to glory. That's what she wanted. Her mama said, "I want to go out hearing Ditty Blaylock's songs and I hope when I meet Jesus, they will be playing a Ditty Blaylock song up in heaven, too." Isn't that just precious? Touched my heart all the way clear to my soul. Can you imagine if my music is playing up in heaven? That'd be better than any award I've ever won.

ABIGAIL. Yes...that would be...just...wonderful.

DITTY. You don't sound sincere. What did I teach you? To say things with conviction, even if you don't mean them.

ABIGAIL. Which is a form of lying, isn't it?

DITTY. Oh no. It's a form of kindness. To make people think they matter, that what they say is important. Nothing wrong with a little acting to sell what you are saying. I don't believe that would constitute real lying...when kindness is involved. Oh! Your pills! It's time for your pills. I promised that good doctor with the Indian name too hard to pronounce that I would make sure you got them on time.

ABIGAIL. Dr. Acharya. Yes, they still follow your directions, "Keep Abigail and her anger issues under control. Do whatever it takes."

DITTY. Yes. Let's see... (Reading the pill bottle.) Two every six hours. (Looks at watch.) Gave you two at noon and it's 6:01. Almost to the minute. Oh, I forgot water –

ABIGAIL. I can dry swallow. I never need water.

DITTY. Good! Saves me another trip to the kitchen.

> *(She hands* **ABIGAIL** *two pills.* **ABIGAIL** *downs them, dry swallows.)*

My old hip hurts like the dickens sometimes. Especially when it gets cold. I hope I don't have to have it replaced, like Lucille Dobson...'member Lucille? She stood on her feet behind that bank window for as far back as I remember. Never changed her hairdo but had that hip replacement and was back at work in a month.

Thought it was neuralgia, but her joints were bone to bone. *(Distant.)* Do you have good memories, Midl' Sis? Rachel says she has a hard time remembering the good memories. I have so many good memories, Abigail. Myself, I do, I have them.

ABIGAIL. *(Long pause.)* I do. Yes, I do. But...well, so many of the good memories became bad memories.

DITTY. Well, that makes not one lick of sense. Just like exercise. *(Stands and looks out.)* Look at your baby sister out there just running around the property like that nasty hamster you and Rachel convinced me to let y'all have. Just going nowhere. *(Pause.)* Good memories remain good memories forever, just like bad memories stay bad memories.

ABIGAIL. They can turn bad, Mama. Remember when we got our first tour bus and we were so happy –

DITTY. Living on high cotton. Buck Owens sold me that bus, way lower than its value because Buck loved the Lord, and I think he mighta been a little sweet on your mama.

ABIGAIL. You, Rachel, Beth – and Jude all on the road together. There were once...once there were so many good memories on that bus, us practicing, then singing for big churches, events...opening for sweet Sandi Patty –

DITTY. Tucker Davis reached out to her to be on the special, but she has a conflict in Dallas. Best voice in gospel music! I won't say that publicly, but I'll say it to you. When I imagine angels singing, it's a choir of Sandi Pattys.

ABIGAIL. *(Remembering.)* That bus...that's where me and Jude fell in love. Everybody would go to bed, including us, then we'd sneak back up –

DITTY. I did not know that! *(A joke.)* Well, too late to punish you now.

ABIGAIL. We held hands for the first time on that bus and Jude kissed me for the first time on that bus. I was seventeen, he was nineteen. He knew what he was doing and had to teach me. But I sure caught on. And it was when we were kissing...when everybody was asleep that he tried –

DITTY. Tried to what?

ABIGAIL. Tried to make love to me, Mama. I mean, come on. We were teenagers with raging hormones. But I held on to it...my virginity...just like you taught us. "They won't buy the cow if they can get the milk for free." Then... when they got back from Las Vegas...married...just left the tour bus after our show in Sacramento, came back expecting us... I'm not sure what they expected... but all those memories on the bus, Mama. All those good memories...the ones in every church, where I'd look over during our show, more than once and catch Jude's eye and we traded that look...that love look...that look that nobody has ever looked at me again with... *(Long pause.)* And I wonder...on the bus...during my good memories...was Rachel...did she get up after I went to bed? When did they start? Was it going on for months...years? Where? What city? Did they trade love looks...they had to have traded love looks, too, because...out of nowhere, it seemed, out of nowhere... but it couldn't have been out of nowhere... Did she give him the milk for free? Was that why he...? Maybe you were wrong about that, Mama. *(Tears perhaps.)* So, yes, Mama, good memories can turn to bad memories when your mind starts up, starts wondering...fillin' in blanks of what you don't know...wondering. And she...and he ruined almost every good memory I had.

(**DITTY** *reaches over and takes* **ABIGAIL***'s hand.*)

DITTY. I understand now –

ABIGAIL. You do?

DITTY. Yes. Did that...did telling me all that make you angry?

ABIGAIL. *(Smiles weakly.)* No Mama. The pills...they work. No more anger issues for Abigail Dorothy Blaylock.

DITTY. I gave you my name. You're my namesake. I almost forgot that. Dorothy. The name I never used. Ditty is such a silly name, but I just love it because it makes me think of my dear, sweet papa. Nicknamed me that because I wrote little "ditties"...songs... I wrote my first song, my first little "ditty" when I was just three years old. Did you know that?

ABIGAIL. I did. You've told that story many, many times. *(Softly.)* I wonder why I never saw them exchange love looks.

(**BETHANY** *enters the living room front door in shorts and a tank top, dripping wet with sweat after her run. A car is heard approaching as she heads up the stairs to the porch.*)

BETHANY. Mama! Rachel's back!

DITTY. Oh Lord!

BETHANY. She's pulling up right now.

DITTY. Thank you, Lil' Sis.

(**BETHANY** *rushes back into the family room, looks out the door.*)

BETHANY. *(Mumbles.)* Shit –

(*On the porch,* **DITTY** *takes a deep breath, gets up, and fiddles with* **ABIGAIL***'s robe.*)

DITTY. We need to get you some new clothes. This tattered ol' robe has seen better days.

ABIGAIL. I like it. It's comfortable.

DITTY. Well, there is something to feeling comfortable. Lord, when I discovered muumuus on the QVC, changed my life. Wish I was back in one now. You want to come down and see if we can all visit –?

ABIGAIL. No… I think I'll just stay here and have a cigarette. I'd probably say something that lacked conviction.

DITTY. Okay, but I wish… *(Mutters.)* Well, I wish so much.

(**DITTY** *exits the porch as* **RACHEL** *storms into the family room and pushes past* **BETHANY***.*)

RACHEL. *(Yelling.)* Ditty Blaylock!! DITTY BLAYLOCK!!!

(**DITTY** *starts down the stairs.*)

DITTY. Good Lord, quit bellowerin' like a cow in heat. Why are you yelling at me –?

RACHEL. Oh just shut up, so I can say what I have to say!

(**RACHEL** *storms to the bottom of the stairs with a mission.*)

ABIGAIL!!! Bethany…where –

BETHANY. Yeah?

RACHEL. *(Turns.)* Oh there you are.

(*ABIGAIL gets up and nervously takes a long drag from her cigarette, then exits the porch and stands at the top of the stairs, holding her cigarette out the porch door, glancing quickly at Jude's door.* **RACHEL** *glares at her for a moment.*)

So, I drove and drove...all the way to Knoxville and back...thinking...and I have made a decision. I will sing for your special, Mama –

DITTY. Praise the Lord! God has answered my prayers.

RACHEL. God had nothing to do with this! (*Deep breath, composes herself.*) So, yes, I will sing. But I have one condition! (*Points at* **ABIGAIL**.) You keep *her* away from me!

(**RACHEL** *goes and gets* **DITTY**'s *gun, loads it as she speaks.*)

I will sleep with my door locked... (*Back to* **DITTY**.) and I'm keeping your gun with me at all times. Loaded!

DITTY. Lord, you are so dramatic!

RACHEL. SHUT! UP! We are not safe! You caused this because of your ridiculous ego. And yes, I will sing – (*Pointedly to* **ABIGAIL**.) but I will shoot if I have to! (*To* **DITTY**.) And then I will expose the truth...*all* of the truth to everybody! And I mean it! (*To* **ABIGAIL**.) You stay away from me, and you stay away from Jude! (*To* **DITTY**.) And this...*this* is the last thing I will ever feel the need to do for you, Mama! Ever!

DITTY. (*Pause. Then, excited.*) Okay, then. We have a plan!

(*Blackout.*)

ACT TWO

Scene One

(Day four. Late afternoon.)

*(Family room. Lights up on **RACHEL**, sitting on the couch obsessed with her computer – or at least pretending to be. The gun sits on the coffee table by the computer. **BETHANY** [or **DITTY**] sits at the piano, playing, **ABIGAIL** and **DITTY** [or **BETHANY**] standing behind. **DITTY** fills in vocally for **RACHEL**. **DITTY** is back in her wig and another bright pantsuit. They are rehearsing "City Of Gold." **RACHEL** looks up and glares at **DITTY**, then **ABIGAIL** occasionally. Tension permeates the room.)*

DITTY, ABIGAIL & BETHANY.
THERE'S A CITY THAT LOOKS O'ER THE VALLEY OF DEATH.
AND ITS GLORY HAS NEVER BEEN TOLD.
WHERE THE LAMB IS THE LIGHT, IN THE MIDST OF THE NIGHT,
IN THAT BEAUTIFUL CITY OF GOLD.

DITTY. *(Claps.)* Good, good. Getting there. Rachel. Honey bunch. Please, pretty please, pretty please come over here and join us so that we can rehearse properly.

RACHEL. I'll join later. I'm uploading my latest episode of "Good Christian Women." There are women who depend on me, Mama. *(Checks computer.)* Looks like... seven minutes to go. You can wait seven more minutes, can't you?

39

DITTY. *(A look to* **ABIGAIL** *and* **BETHANY**.*)* Yes. Far be it from me to diminish the importance of those wonderful sermonettes that you give all those women sitting at home just waiting...waiting with bated breath, sitting at their computers, to hear what you have to say about life and such.

RACHEL. Ten minutes!

DITTY. Oh, don't be like that! *(Sweeter, pleading.)* But Big Sis, we have less than one week before my special and everything is coming together. Thank you all for accepting my invitation to reunite to be a part of the tribute that GMT is giving your mama...honoring your only mama for fifty years in the ministry. Oh, I don't think I told you, Rachel. *(No response.)* Rachel!

     *(***RACHEL** *looks up.)*

Tucker Davis... *(To* **ABIGAIL** *and* **BETHANY**.*)* Tucker's the producer of my special...well, Tucker called me on my cellular phone late last night and...are you ready... Sandi Patty was able to cancel her singing engagement in Dallas...some Baptist convention, something or another, real important...and she will be there and has agreed to sing the big hit I wrote for her that won her yet another Dove Award for Best Gospel Female Performance, I forget what year –

ABIGAIL. She's singing "Jesus Wait For Me, I'm Coming Soon"?

DITTY. Yes!! Yes!!! Oh, Midl' Sis, that means so much that you remembered that –

ABIGAIL. I loved Sandi Patty. She was always kind and sweet to us.

     *(***RACHEL** *glares at* **ABIGAIL**.*)*

DITTY. Well, why wouldn't she be? Your mama wrote her one of her biggest hits. Canceled a high-paying engagement because of her devotion to me.

(**RACHEL** *rolls her eyes.*)

BETHANY. Mama, do you really believe that God built a city of gold and that the sun really never sets and the leaves really never fade? I mean, I like my sleep so I would want the sun to set in heaven and fall is my favorite season. Leaves are so pretty during the fall. Sweater weather. Seems that gold leaves would be more appropriate for a city of gold. *(To* **RACHEL** *and* **ABIGAIL.***)* Did we even know what we were singing when we were little?

DITTY. Lil' Sis. Oh! Your mind! Please do not take us down this road, not now, please, or we'll never get back! This was the Blaylock Sisters' first big hit and our fans will expect it! It's a song with perfect three-part harmony. Please do not dissect the words. You're an atheist. Why do you care about the specifics of heaven when you don't even plan to be there? Big Sis, get on over here, please! These other stars, Carrie, Shirley, Sandi Patty – oh and yes, we *are* letting Larry Gatlin perform after all, but with his brothers, so it'll tie in with your reunion. Tucker says that's good press. The Blaylock *Sisters* and the Gatlin *Brothers* reunite for "The Ditty Blaylock Fifty Years Of Serving Jesus Special." Tucker thought of that. He is a go-getter, I'll give him that. And so handsome. But my point...what was my point –?

BETHANY. That atheists don't go to heaven?

DITTY. No, not that point. We've moved on from that point –

ABIGAIL. That Rachel needs to practice with us.

(**RACHEL** *looks up, glares.*)

DITTY. Yes, that's it! Those other stars...well, trust me they will be well rehearsed because they are professionals. Except Shirley Caesar, who sometimes just goes off on her own odd tangent...says the spirit is leading her. Hmph! Well, I saw the spirit once lead her to pick up a microphone stand and drag it on her back like a cross. Made no sense. A black woman portraying Christ dragging a cross to Golgotha, while singing the entire time! That was not the spirit, I assure you. That was Shirley being theatrical! *(Confused.)* My point?! What was my point? Oh...that they sing...the other stars who have aligned...they sing on a regular basis still, unlike the three of you. They are most likely practicing their Ditty Blaylock song as we speak. You need to practice! That's my point! All of you. A trio means three!

RACHEL. Oh brother. As we speak? Dear Lord, your ego, Mama. And I said I would be there in a few minutes to rehearse. We have a week. People depend on me, Mama. It's not just about you, okay? And I sing on a regular basis too...on my show...at church...around the house...so maybe the girls need extra rehearsal.

ABIGAIL. I sing at the mental institution. For the other mental patients. Calms me down. Calms them down.

DITTY. *(Looks at her watch.)* Yes, and your medication also calms you down. Not due for another fifteen minutes. *(To BETHANY and RACHEL.)* I was given strict instructions on when to issue Abigail's medication. *(For RACHEL's benefit.)* Keeps her calm and sweet.

RACHEL. *(Mutters.)* Does it also keep her from strangling people?

(Uncomfortable silence.)

ABIGAIL. *(Tentative.)* Rachel, I feel...well, I feel that we need to talk, to hash things out –

DITTY. No! We don't! We need to sing! To practice! Just let Rachel pout like a titty baby! Maybe I'll go make her a sugar tit to suck on. *(No response.)* I'm glad you have been singing, Abigail...that you can use your God-given talent...for a ministry, well, a ministry of sorts at Meadowbrook.

ABIGAIL. We have church on Sundays. Lots there were raised just like me. Us. In the church. There's this one guy, he's from Tennessee somewhere. His dad was a preacher, so he preaches. David. Biblical name, of course. Just like us. He doesn't make much sense since he's bat-shit crazy –

DITTY. Language, language –

ABIGAIL. Sorry. But I do sing. It calms so many of them down. It calms me down.

BETHANY. I hate my name.

DITTY. What?! You have a beautiful name! Why on earth are you bringing that up –?

BETHANY. Do you believe in God, Abigail? I don't.

DITTY. She does. And please keep that to yourself! I'm sorry I brought it up. If that word got out, they'd cancel my tribute so fast it'd make your head spin.

RACHEL. Oh Bethany, please let that get out! Let everything get out! If it means this nightmare will end, please just go straight to the press!

DITTY. What? No! We have to stay the course, not get sidetracked. She's not really an atheist, she's just going through a phase.

RACHEL. You should hear about the other phase she's going through.

BETHANY. Stop! Let's get back to this song!

DITTY. What'd I miss? Did I miss something?

RACHEL. Why don't you ask Bethany about her sex life, Mama?

DITTY. Dear Lord in heaven! Why on earth would I want to know about that?

BETHANY. I think we need to practice. That uploaded yet?

(A "stop it" look to **RACHEL.***)*

RACHEL. I don't know, Mama. You seem to be obsessed with mine.

DITTY. That's because it's sick, Rachel. Making love to a man in a coma who should be in heaven with our Lord and Savior is just plain sick!

(**ABIGAIL** *looks up the stairs.*)

RACHEL. Oh, just you wait!

BETHANY. Rachel –!!!

DITTY. (*To* **ABIGAIL** *and* **BETHANY.**) And she is very loud! (*Back to* **RACHEL.**) Keeping him alive artificially is just wrong. If medicine and science had been around during Biblical times, I'm sure there would have been a scripture about that.

ABIGAIL. (*Fighting anxiety.*) Soothing music. Soothing music. Soothing music. (*Looks up the stairs, too loud.*) Mama, music... That one particular thing, I so am grateful to you for, Mama.

DITTY. Well, thank you, that means so much, Abigail. Now is everybody clear on their parts? It's all floodin' back, isn't it? I knew it would. Like riding a bicycle. Any questions?

BETHANY. Why did you name the other girls after people in the Bible. And you named me after a small village –

DITTY. Oh dear Lord in heaven. Your mind! Just jumps around like one of those Mexican jumping beans! Always have and always will just think of the most ridiculous things to question. Wanting to sleep...the four seasons in heaven. Now this! You expect me to remember that far back? Bethany is a pretty name. That's why. It's a pretty Biblical name.

(**ABIGAIL**'s *anxiety increases. She looks at the sheet music, hums, reaches over* **BETHANY**, *pecks out her part, hums more, paces, looks* *up the stairs.* **RACHEL** *watches her every move.)*

BETHANY. But it's the name of a town. Maybe that's why I was so fat as a child. You named me after an entire village!

DITTY. A very small village! And that had nothing to do with it. You ate like a little piggy is why...and you were not fat, you were fleshy! We really need to practice –

> **(ABIGAIL** *looks up from the music, more anxiety, looks upstairs toward Jude's room, pecks more notes, paces, hums her part.* **DITTY** *watches her, worried. She takes out the bottle of pills from her pocket, places it on the dining table, looks at her watch, during:)*

BETHANY. I was fat, not fleshy –

RACHEL. *(Overlap.)* Oh yes, drop everything...back to the picture!

BETHANY. *(Overlap.)* And I was named after a village.

RACHEL. *(Overlap.)* I'll just go over here and be the frame with the other Blaylock Sisters so Mama can be the picture, the star...and we'll be supporting characters... for her big, big special on GMT...where all the stars are aligning...framing her too... Carrie Underwood, Vince Gill, Amy Grant, Larry Asshole Gatlin –

DITTY. Rachel! Language!

RACHEL. Even Shirley Caesar who has forgiven Mama for being a racist will be there.

DITTY. I am not a racist!

> **(ABIGAIL**'s *anxiety increases. She paces more, hums some of her part.)*

RACHEL. Oh yes you are!

DITTY. I'm from the South!

ABIGAIL. *(Quiet desperation, singing.)*
THERE'S A CITY THAT LOOKS O'ER THE VALLEY OF DEATH,
AND ITS GLORY HAS NEVER BEEN TOLD.

BETHANY. Let's just practice! *(Whispers, indicates* **ABIGAIL.***)*
Look!

> *(They all stare at* **ABIGAIL,** *who is now standing on the landing by the porch door, pounding on it to the beat of the song.)*

ABIGAIL. *(Loudly singing her part, very rushed.)*
WHERE THE LAMB IS THE LIGHT,
IN THE MIDST OF THE NIGHT,
IN THAT BEAUTIFUL CITY OF GOLD.

DITTY. *(Pause, a look of concern, then loudly.)* That's perfect, Midl' Sis! *(Loudly.)* What are you looking for up there, sweet pea?

ABIGAIL. I need a cigarette! *(Sings, almost frantically.)*
THERE'S A CITY THAT LOOKS O'ER THE VALLEY OF DEATH.

RACHEL. I thought she was fine now, Mama. Rehabilitated. That we are not in danger!

> **(ABIGAIL** *stands at the top of the stairs, glances at Jude's room.)*

ABIGAIL. I just get anxious without my cigarettes. Mama said I couldn't smoke while we practice.

DITTY. You need to quit. It's a nasty, nasty habit that has aged you, and you will die a horrible death of cancer.

ABIGAIL. *(Screaming.)* I LIKE TO SMOKE!!! *(Catches herself.)* Sorry. *(Almost whispers.)* I like to smoke. It's one of the pleasures of life I still get to enjoy.

DITTY. Okay, then. Please! Can we just practice –?

RACHEL. For the record, Mama, you are so much more than a racist!

(**DITTY** *storms over to* **RACHEL.**)

DITTY. And you tell me not to judge! Do you not ever have the ability to be wrong?

(**BETHANY** *starts laughing.*)

RACHEL. Do you?! *(To* **BETHANY.***)* What's so funny?

BETHANY. You. Mama. Still arguing. It's just funny...and refreshing. Family. You know. *(Laughs harder.)* Remember that time, we all got tickled...over that woman who was baptized...that real fat woman –

DITTY. Dalinda Baker! Died a horrible death.

ABIGAIL. *(Suddenly breaks from anxious spell.)* Yes! Yes! *(Starts laughing too, comes downstairs.)* I remember! We all got the church giggles! And Mama, you pinched us so hard.

DITTY. Or was that Carmelita Woods who gave you girls that nasty hamster. Her youngest son, you know, is now in the pen over in Ashland for sellin' dope. The one with that smooshed-in face. Looks like it's not quite done. Needs to go back in the oven for about ten minutes on high.

ABIGAIL. It was Dalinda! And the water started sloshing out! We were really little and Bethany, you started... started laughing...and then me and Rachel chimed in... but you always had that that little snort, Beth...and Mama pinched us one by one...you last...and you yelled out, "Mama, stop pinchin' me! That hurts."

DITTY. *(Joins the laughter.)* Oh, Lord, I've never been so embarrassed in all my life.

(**ABIGAIL** *and* **BETHANY** *howl, but one by one they stop as they notice that* **RACHEL** *is not* *laughing, as if she didn't hear, fixed on the computer.)*

DITTY. *(To* ABIGAIL *and* BETHANY.*)* Well...alright then... that was a fun stroll down memory lane. *(For* RACHEL*'s benefit.)* A good memory for most of us. But now, now we must practice. Rachel –

RACHEL. I know my part! I can jump in later! Leave me alone until I finish my work. It's not always all about you, Ditty Blaylock! And maybe, just maybe Sandi Patty was sweet and kind to us because she is sweet and kind by nature and it had nothing to do with you writing her biggest hit.

DITTY. This is what I have to live with, what I have to listen to, day in, day out. *(False emotion.)* No respect whatsoever... Just says the meanest things and hurts my feelings to the core of my soul. Daily!

(DITTY *goes and sits in her chair, pouting.* RACHEL *storms over.)*

RACHEL. What do you not get, Mama?! *I know my part.* And I haven't been paid like the other two! And Bethany is the best singer, remember? So, *you* sing my part until I can get over there. It's that easy. So please, please just shut up while I upload this latest episode, or put a check in my hand and I promise to get over there to your practice session faster!

(RACHEL *returns to the sofa.)*

DITTY. Done! In fact, I'll give you cold, hard cash!

(DITTY *rushes over to the gun drawer, opens it, and angrily grabs a wad of cash out of it, then storms back over to* RACHEL *and starts counting the bills and stacking them in five stacks of one thousand each.)*

One, two, three, four, five, six, seven, eight, nine, ten.
One thousand! One, two, three, four, five, six, seven,
eight, nine, ten. Two thousand! One, two, three, four,
five, six, seven, eight, nine, ten. Three thousand. One,
two, three, four, five, six, seven, eight, nine, ten. Four
thousand. One, two, three, four, five, six, seven, eight,
nine, ten. Five thousand! PAID IN FULL!

> (**DITTY** *storms back to the gun box and throws
> some remaining bills into it.* **RACHEL** *takes in
> her money, stores it inside her computer, then
> slams the computer shut. She takes her place
> by the piano. As she passes* **DITTY,** *she gives
> her a look.)*

(Chokes up.) Oh Big Sis, Midl' Sis, Little Sis. We're
back together again. The Blaylock Sisters. America is
going to be just beside themselves. I mean all those...
other stars...that lineup...it will be monumental... But
oh darlin's, the highlight will be the Blaylock Sisters
together again with me just beaming with pride as you
sing. People are just going to weep! I know I will. I
hope they capture that on camera. They are just going
to flat-out weep buckets. Now let's practice!

> (**BETHANY** *[or* **DITTY***] plays a rousing
> introduction to "City Of Gold," and the
> Blaylock Sisters sing in perfect three-part
> harmony.)*

RACHEL, ABIGAIL & BETHANY.
THERE'S A CITY THAT LOOKS O'ER THE VALLEY OF DEATH.
AND ITS GLORY HAS NEVER BEEN TOLD.
WHERE THE LAMB IS THE LIGHT, IN THE MIDST OF THE
NIGHT,
IN THAT BEAUTIFUL CITY OF GOLD.

DITTY. *(Overlap.)* Good, good!

BETHANY.
WHERE THE SUN.

RACHEL & ABIGAIL.
WHERE THE SUN.

BETHANY.
NEVER SETS.

DITTY. *(Overlap.)* Just wonderful!

RACHEL & ABIGAIL.
NEVER SETS.

BETHANY.
AND THE LEAVES.

RACHEL & ABIGAIL.
AND THE LEAVES.

BETHANY.
NEVER FADE.

RACHEL, ABIGAIL & BETHANY.
WHERE THE RIGHTEOUS FOREVER WILL SHINE LIKE THE STARS,
IN THAT BEAUTIFUL CITY OF GOLD.

DITTY. *(Overlap.)* Oh, yes!

> (**RACHEL** *turns and glares at* **ABIGAIL** *as they begin the second verse, then is irritated as* **DITTY** *pats her in approval.)*

RACHEL.
THERE WILL BE NO MORE SORROW, PAIN, SICKNESS OR DEATH.

DITTY. Perfect!

BETHANY.
AND THE SAINTS THERE WILL NEVER GROW OLD.

DITTY. Still the best singer!

(RACHEL *shoots a look at* DITTY.)

ABIGAIL.
HOW I LONG FOR THAT CITY, WHERE THERE NEVER
   COMES A NIGHT.

DITTY. Oh, Abigail, lovely!

RACHEL, ABIGAIL & BETHANY.
IN THAT BEAUTIFUL CITY OF GOLD.
WHERE THE SUN, NEVER –"

> (RACHEL *can no longer contain herself. She
> screams, reaches over* BETHANY *[or* DITTY*],
> and slams both hands on the piano over and
> over.* DITTY *lets out a scream as everything
> comes to an abrupt stop.*)

RACHEL. *(To* DITTY.*)* How are we supposed to just talk?
(Turns on ABIGAIL.*)* Hash it out? It's not like me...like
me stealing your precious lavender bow in Shreveport!
I'm just not sure how you saying, "Sorry I put Jude in a
coma for the past twenty-five years" is going to resolve –

DITTY. Rachel, stop it!

RACHEL. You may have covered it up to the world, Mama,
but you did not cover it up for us!

DITTY. You cannot go to that place!

RACHEL. I can and I will and I just did! *(Back to* ABIGAIL.*)*
You should be in jail, not an institution... *(Back to*
DITTY.*)* and then she couldn't get out to do your stupid
tribute!

DITTY. Stupid –?

BETHANY. *(Overlap.)* Y'all! It was going so –

ABIGAIL. *(Overlap.)* I need a cigarette –

BETHANY. *(Overlap.)* ...Good.

ABIGAIL. And I do not have to listen –

(ABIGAIL *starts to walk up the stairs, but*
RACHEL *goes and grabs her arm.*)

RACHEL. Oh, yes you do! *(To* BETHANY.*)* And it was not
going good! We were pretending and I refuse to
pretend so Mama can have another moment of glory!

ABIGAIL. *(Pulls her arm away.)* Let go of me!

(RACHEL *rushes around* ABIGAIL, *blocking
the stairs.*)

DITTY. Big Sis, please –!

RACHEL. This has been bottled up inside of me for years
and –!

BETHANY. But it was so long ago –

DITTY. Yes, water under the –

RACHEL. Water under the bridge for strangling my husband?
She all but murdered the love of my life –!

ABIGAIL. *(Losing it.)* He was the love of *my* life, you fuckin'
bitch –!

*(Note: Overlaps. Respect the lines, not the
cues.)*

DITTY. Oh dear, that word!

ABIGAIL. That you stole –

RACHEL. No, he chose me over you –

ABIGAIL. Because you threw yourself at him –

RACHEL. I did not! LIAR!!!

ABIGAIL. Like a goddamn whore –!!

DITTY. Not the Lord's name in vain –!

RACHEL. He started the whole thing, not me –

ABIGAIL. YOU'RE THE LIAR! LIAR!

RACHEL. Because he didn't love you anymore –

ABIGAIL. LIAR!!

RACHEL. He loved me!

DITTY. Don't push her there. She has anger issues...

ABIGAIL. You stole my lavender bow and you stole –!

DITTY. It's pill time! *(Shakes bottle of pills.)* Pill time, Abigail –!!!

ABIGAIL. *(Rushing* DITTY.*)* NO! I don't want those goddamn pills. I want to –

DITTY. Well, you have to obey the doctor's –

ABIGAIL. Feel!

DITTY. ...Orders.

ABIGAIL. I don't need pills... I need to feel this!

DITTY. Oh, this has taken a bad turn –

RACHEL. No shit, Mama! Yeah, I can cuss too! NO...umm... No...FUCKIN' SHIT! See? I have anger issues too!

DITTY. Oh dear Lord! What would your good Christian women think on that internet –? Abigail, here's your –

ABIGAIL. I'm not taking the pills, Mama! I'm done! I want to go back! Fuck this fuckin' shit!

> *(*ABIGAIL *heads to the front door.)*

DITTY. Let's just get you your medicine!

ABIGAIL. *(Overlap.)* I don't want any fuckin' pills!

> *(She grabs the bottle from* DITTY *and throws it, pills going everywhere. Quietly crying,* BETHANY *picks up the bottle and starts picking up the pills as* ABIGAIL *storms out the door,* RACHEL *on her heels.)*

RACHEL. No, you are here now and you are going to hear what I have to say!

(*ABIGAIL drives* RACHEL *back into the house. She has snapped!*)

ABIGAIL. (*Exploding.*) FUCK YOU! FUCK YOU, RACHEL! Jude is in a coma because of you! Because you stole –

DITTY. (*Clapping her hands together.*) Stop it!!!

ABIGAIL. ...My fiancé. You went after him and were determined to take the LOVE OF MY FUCKIN' LIFE, YOU FUCKIN' BITCH! I should have strangled you, not him. That's my one regret!

DITTY. Stop it this instant!

RACHEL. Oh shut up, Mama! This is what you deserve!

BETHANY. (*Crying.*) Y'all, please, please, please –

RACHEL. And she's no longer dangerous –?!

DITTY. We just need to get her her pills!

ABIGAIL. I'M NOT TAKING ANY MORE FUCKING PILLS! Because I want to feel! I want to be real. The real me... So, yes, oh yes, I'm still plenty dangerous, Big Sis! So you better watch it, because I've been locked up for twenty-five fuckin' years, my life ripped away from me...and I'm boiling inside! Because of you! And now I'm here, with anger issues like...like...oh like you, have no fuckin' idea, so you better sleep with one fuckin' eye open!

(*She pushes* RACHEL *aside and rushes up the stairs.* RACHEL *bounds up the stairs after her, spewing:*)

RACHEL. YOU BITCH! YOU CRAZY BITCH!!! I'M NOT SCARED OF YOU. I WILL –

DITTY. (*Overlap.*) Oh dear sweet Jesus! That language! Like a cable movie!

(Landing. **ABIGAIL** *heads to the porch,* **RACHEL** *on her heels. She then turns and pushes past* **RACHEL**, *opens the bedroom door, sees Jude, gasps, quickly turns, and locks the door as* **RACHEL** *reaches it.* **RACHEL** *tries to open it, realizes it's locked.)*

RACHEL. Open this door! Mama! She's in there with Jude! Open this door, open this door, open this door!!!

(But **ABIGAIL** *is fixed on Jude, not hearing* **RACHEL**. *She starts walking toward him, and as the lights slowly fade, she climbs on him and straddles him.)*

Open this door! Open this door! Mama, she's in there with Jude. Get the key!

DITTY. *(Overlap.)* Where is it –?!

RACHEL. In the kitchen!

*(**DITTY** rushes into the kitchen;* **RACHEL** *rushes down the stairs, exits into the kitchen.)*

Mama, this is your fault. Get the key! *(Offstage.)* Get the key!!!

*(**ABIGAIL** stares at Jude and sweetly touches his face.)*

ABIGAIL. *(Softly.)* Oh, Jude.

(Blackout.)

Scene Two

(Day four. Thirty minutes later.)

*(Bedroom. Lights on **RACHEL** turning Jude, straightening his bedding. She changes his feeding bag, then works his legs and arms, massaging his muscles.)*

*(Porch. Lights on **ABIGAIL**, smoking and rocking.)*

*(Family room. Lights on **BETHANY** as she sets the table for four.)*

*(**DITTY** walks up the stairs, onto the porch.)*

DITTY. How are you feeling, Midl' Sis?

ABIGAIL. *(Emotional.)* Better now. Thank you. I'm sorry.

DITTY. All done. All over. Over and done with. We are now in the calm after the storm. The *only* storm. Those pills kick in yet? The doctor said they should kick in within thirty minutes. *(Checks her wristwatch.)* It's almost been that.

ABIGAIL. I'm not sure. I think so. You were right. I shouldn'ta... I didn't need to feel. *(Quietly.)* Not that. Didn't need to feel that.

DITTY. I agree. Sometimes it's just best to suppress feelings and not express them. Oh look, I made a rhyme without even trying. Maybe I could write songs again. *(Watches **ABIGAIL** smoke, waves the air again.)* Well, do you feel calmer? Is the anger gone? Seems it. Needs to be gone, Midl' Sis.

ABIGAIL. Yes, ma'am. I'm sorry. Please tell Rachel I'm sorry and that nothing happened in there. I just saw him. Just saw him, I touched his face...nothing...nothing else happened.

DITTY. We know nothing happened. Wasn't time for... before she got that door opened, but...what were you thinking...what were you intending? *(No answer.)* Never mind. I do not want or need to know. It's all over now. You girls said some harsh words, but...maybe what was needed to be said has been said. *(Mutters.)* Could have been said without all that vulgar language. I did not raise you girls to talk like truckers. But what's done is done. And we are human, Midl' Sis. Flawed human beings. If we weren't, we wouldn't need Jesus to wipe away our sins. If we didn't sin, then Jesus died for nothing.

ABIGAIL. I think more needs to be said. I need to tell Rachel my truth...all of it. You taught us to tell the truth –

DITTY. I did. The truth shall set you free. John 8:32.

ABIGAIL. *(Laughs.)* Ironic, since you locked me up, Mama.

> *(This stumps* **DITTY.***)*

The truth did not set me free, Mama! It got me locked up in the loony bin and you hold the key! *(Getting angrier.)* They lied to me! They lied to all of us! And then they just thought...they could come back... married? I mean, who does that? What did they think my reaction would be, Mama?

DITTY. I don't know, but I'm fairly sure it did not involve strangulation. And please, calm down. I wonder if I should give you an extra dose of medication.

ABIGAIL. No! They've kicked in! No more pills. I'll...stay... calm. I promise. And yes ma'am, I'm fairly certain too, it did not involve... *(Softly.)* strangulation. Yes...that... that...was a big mistake. Understatement to say the least.

> *(***DITTY** *goes over and waters a hanging basket.* **ABIGAIL** *gets up and follows her.)*

ABIGAIL. And if I could take back one moment in time, Mama...a granted wish or something like in the stories you used to read us, well, of course, I'd choose that one. *(Pause, distant.)* And he...she...no matter what they did to me...did not deserve that. I do know that. *(Pause.)* So, I live my punishment daily, which will never be enough. You locked me up, you kept me out of prison and I have never been angry at you for that. You threw away the key to my life, but I'm not angry at you. But her...him...yes, I'm so very mad still. *(Sighs.)* And even if she forgave me...could I forgive her? Forgiveness is a slippery slope, Mama. Is it really that important?

> *(Bedroom. **RACHEL** gets up and starts to exit, starts to descend the stairs, hears the voices, changes her mind, and pauses on the landing, listening by the door.)*

DITTY. I believe it is. The Bible says it is.

ABIGAIL. Seven times seventy. That's how much the Bible says we're supposed to forgive. That's a lot of forgiveness if you ask me. Maybe Jesus was a stutterer like Billy Dobbs was in high school. Jesus probably said...ssss... seven and some hard-of-hearing asshole disciple wrote down seventy times seven.

DITTY. Oh, please don't call Jesus' disciples that ugly word.

ABIGAIL. Sorry. Even seven's a lot. Sometimes it's just too much to ask for. I don't expect Rachel...or Jude...if he was capable...to forgive me for what I did 'cause, *that* was a crime. That was one big crime...and even if he were capable of forgiveness...why should he? I took his... *(Lost in thought.)* life...without taking his life. *(Tears perhaps.)* And even if everybody forgave....Jude will still be...gone.

DITTY. Yes. And he doesn't deserve to just lay there like a vegetable, day in, day out. I haven't been up there to see him for years. I just want to remember...the good memories...that sweet boy. *(Chokes up.)* But you are right, Abigail...they have been tainted and changed.

ABIGAIL. Will you go see if Rachel will please... I'll be calm, I promise.

> (**RACHEL** *stops eavesdropping and rushes down the stairs.*)

(More emotional.) Maybe if she could forgive, I could get there too. Oh, Mama, I'd love to be able to forgive. I know life will never be the same, but I'd like to be able to –

DITTY. *(Sighs.)* Okay.

ABIGAIL. Thank you –

> (**DITTY** *exits the porch, starts to walk down the stairs, then looks at Jude's room, makes a decision, opens the bedroom door, enters, and stares at him for a moment.*)

> (*Family room.* **RACHEL** *sits on the couch, changes the location of the gun, still on the coffee table, and opens the laptop as* **BETHANY** *enters with silverware. She stares at* **RACHEL,** *places the silver on the table, then goes over and turns on the porch light and a lamp.*)

BETHANY. I was going to ask you if you're okay, but I realize that that is a very stupid question. Is Jude okay?

RACHEL. No, Bethany. He's in a coma.

> (*Bedroom.* **DITTY**'s *eyes fill with tears at the sight. She shakes her head, then quickly exits.*)

BETHANY. I mean –

RACHEL. I know what you mean. He's back to what he was.

(**DITTY** *walks down the stairs, shaking off the sight of Jude.* **BETHANY** *finishes setting the silverware at the table.*)

DITTY. Well, those pills have kicked in. Hallelujah, praise Jesus! She's calm again.

BETHANY. That's great, Mama.

(**RACHEL** *glares at* **DITTY.** **DITTY** *clocks the gun.*)

DITTY. Don't look at me with that tone of voice. I can't control –

RACHEL. Exactly!

DITTY. Well, your sister would love to talk. Says she's calm and she's sorry, and I think talking in a civilized manner would be –

RACHEL. No. Thanks. I heard…enough. Not interested in hearing more.

DITTY. *(Storms into the kitchen.)* I can't win for losing with you.

BETHANY. Maybe you should –

RACHEL. No!

DITTY. *(Yelling offstage.)* Lil' Sis, how did you make chili so fast? Smells delicious.

BETHANY. *(Calling.)* It's a hybrid. Canned with some creative additions. I had this fantasy that we could all have a meal together.

(**DITTY** *returns with a cup towel.*)

DITTY. Oh, if I had known, I could have whipped up a big skillet of cornbread. Chili is always better with cornbread. Although I do not have any buttermilk and I do not like cornbread with sweet milk.

RACHEL. So what did you expect, Mama? Did you expect us all just to keep our mouths shut and sing –?

DITTY. *(Carefully wording.)* I thought… I thought that for once in all of your lives that you could just put everything aside…for one tiny week for your mama. Just let bygones be bygones for one week –

> (**DITTY** *wanders over to the coffee table and discretely places the towel over the gun.* **RACHEL** *grabs the towel and angrily tosses it aside.*)

RACHEL. Bygones be bygones. Unbelievable.

DITTY. Yes! But of course, as always, my expectations of my children, of my girls, my daughters were just stomped and splattered like an armadillo on a country road. And you wonder why I'm disappointed? And stay depressed most of the time? Have writer's block and cannot write any more songs for Jesus?! And now…I guess…just answer me this one question, Big Sis. Do I need to call Tucker Davis and tell him "no Blaylock Sisters"? Huh? Do I? Do I need to give up the biggest night of my life? The biggest celebration of the career that the good Lord above handed to me and to us?!

> (**RACHEL** *stares at* **DITTY.** *Unbelievable.* **BETHANY** *stares at* **RACHEL,** *then at* **DITTY.**)

BETHANY. *(Blurts out.)* I'm a lesbian –

> (**DITTY** *just stares at* **BETHANY,** *then back at* **RACHEL,** *who bursts out laughing.* **DITTY** *stares hard at* **RACHEL,** *then slowly chooses her words.*)

DITTY. Well, at this point, Lil' Sis – nothing you are or do surprises me. Nothing shocks me. There is no news, nothing, that can rock the foundation of my faith. My house is built on rock, not sand. And if all of this... all of this *horror*...this life of horror...hasn't destroyed me yet, then I am indestructible! I've accomplished so much. Fame and fortune. So many blessings. But I remain unhappy because I have failed! Failed to give my daughters happy lives. So, if...if anybody has a shot, Lil' Sis, it's probably you. Rachel and Abigail are lost causes, but you are not. So, I do not need to understand your being an atheist or a...lesbian... *(Chokes up.)* I just want you to find peace – and happiness...before it's too late.

(**BETHANY** *hugs* **DITTY**.)

BETHANY. I'm trying, Mama. I'm really trying –

(**RACHEL** *stares at them hugging.* **DITTY** *starts to pull away from* **BETHANY**.)

Don't let go, Mama. This feels good.

(*Lights dim on* **ABIGAIL** *as she continues to smoke, then lights dim on* **BETHANY** *and* **DITTY** *hugging as* **RACHEL** *watches.*)

(*Blackout.*)

Scene Three

(Day four. Fifteen minutes later.)

(Kitchen. Lights on the family at the table, **BETHANY** *standing, serving chili from a soup tureen.* **RACHEL** *stares at* **ABIGAIL,** *then* **DITTY,** *then* **BETHANY.)*

DITTY. Well. *(Chokes up.)* Here we are. Together again. Breaking bread. Lil' Sis, thank you for making this meal.

BETHANY. Sure, Mama.

RACHEL. *(Mutters.)* There is no bread.

> *(**DITTY** gets up, rushes to the bread box, grabs a partial loaf of white bread, and slaps it down on the table.)*

DITTY. And now there is!

> *(**BETHANY** sits as **DITTY** returns to her chair. **ABIGAIL** takes a bite of the chili.)*

Now, Midl' Sis – I don't know how they do things over at the...facility...but here we still return thanks.

ABIGAIL. *(Puts her spoon down.)* Yes, ma'am. Sorry. That one bite was real good, Beth –

DITTY. Now who wants to do the honors? I'm assuming you are out of the equation, Bethany. I'm fairly certain that atheists do not pray and I have no earthly idea if lesbians do.

BETHANY. The ones who are atheists don't.

DITTY. Ah-ha. Good to know. *(To* **ABIGAIL.**) Your baby sister is not only an atheist these days but she is now an avowed lesbian. Like Ellen. Which I am trying to be just fine with if she indeed finds happiness. Rachel tells me I don't have an open mind, but I'm here to prove I do. You missed the big announcement while you were smoking and waiting for the pills to kick in upstairs. They have kicked in, haven't they?

ABIGAIL. Yes ma'am.

BETHANY. Chili does not taste good cold.

DITTY. Oh right. Big Sis, you're being very silent there. Just sitting and staring at each one of us, one by one. Makes me a wee bit nervous. Would you like to return thanks?

RACHEL. *(Emphatically.)* No!

DITTY. Well, I guess communication with our Lord and Savior is all up to me. Please, like the reunited family that we are, join hands.

> *(They all join hands.)*

There. Progress. The way it should be. Shall we pray?

> *(All heads bow except BETHANY, who is more than amused during the prayer.)*

Our dear heavenly father. We thank thee for thy bounty and thy love. We thank thee for this chili and the hands of the one who has prepared it. Make her believe again, Lord, make her believe! We thank thee for this reunion and for the opportunity to serve thee with our music one more time. May our music touch and heal hearts, including our own. Amen.

ABIGAIL. Amen.

> *(They all begin to eat, except RACHEL.)*

DITTY. Oh, Lil' Sis. This is divine. Best chili I believe I've ever had. Has a little kick to it.

BETHANY. Thank you. A dash of cayenne pepper.

DITTY. Ah-ha. *(Coughing.)* Yes. I taste that cayenne.

(**DITTY** *gets up, gets a pitcher of tea, and pours all around.*)

RACHEL. So, you want to talk, Abigail?

ABIGAIL. *(Pause.)* Yes. I –

DITTY. Oh, let's just enjoy this meal together and talk after supper. I'm just getting used to the calm and my nerves are barely steady from that last cuss-filled fight.

ABIGAIL. I can stay calm. I will stay calm. I promise to stay calm.

RACHEL. I can stay calm, too.

DITTY. Well, let's all stay calm and talk after supper. Everything will settle better that way –

RACHEL. *(Exploding.)* You don't make the rules, Mama! She wants to talk. I want to talk. We're going to talk! Go out by the creek to your thinking and songwriting spot, take your chili with you if you do not want to listen! Because WE ARE GOING TO TALK!

DITTY. This does not sound calm to me! Does that sound calm to you, Lil' Sis?

RACHEL. Some of us don't stay medicated to stay calm.

BETHANY. I have an idea. When Gail and I were having relationship problems –

DITTY. Gail is a woman I take it?

BETHANY. Yes.

DITTY. Because there are men also named Gale. Brother Gale Ryan, that disgraced evangelist from Tupelo. Prostitutes and dope. I just wanted to be clear.

(**DITTY** *returns to her seat.*)

BETHANY. *(Pointedly.)* This one is a woman. See, Gail and I were trying to make things work out…and me stripping had caused a big problem in our relationship –

DITTY. *(Trying.)* Aha –

BETHANY. So we went back to Dr. Welton, the therapist you used to pay for, Mama –

DITTY. Yes, I remember writing those checks weekly. Outrageous what they charge. That's why God has always been my therapist.

RACHEL. *(Sarcastic.)* Yes, and he's done such a wonderful job.

BETHANY. And he would mediate. I'd say my piece and Gail would say hers. He had this little saying..."Say your piece, but keep your peace."

DITTY. Oh I like that! I need to write that down so I can remember it. There's a song in that, I do believe.

> (**DITTY** *gets up, grabs a pad and pen, then sits again and writes.*)

BETHANY. And him moderating...mediating...really helped us talk...and listen...really listen to each other.

DITTY. Yes! Civil. Keep it civil. I could moderate too.

RACHEL. NO! I want Bethany to moderate and I'd like you to either leave the room or the house or sit there and keep your big, always constantly blabbering, uncensored, droning on, massive mouth shut, Ditty Blaylock!

DITTY. See how she treats me?

> (**DITTY** *gets up, dramatically grabs her bowl of chili, pushes her chair under the table, and storms up the stairs. As she reaches the top, she turns back.*)

Please let me know when I'm welcome to sit at my own table!

(She waits for a response. There is none. She exits down the hallway.)

RACHEL. *(To ABIGAIL.)* Does this work for you?

ABIGAIL. Yes, it works for me.

BETHANY. Okay, let's see. Well, Dr. Welton would ask us to take a moment to collect our thoughts, think about what we need to say to each other.

(ABIGAIL sighs, nervous.)

RACHEL. I'm ready whenever she is. I've been collecting my thoughts of what I need to say for a couple of decades.

ABIGAIL. I need just a moment –

RACHEL. Then is it okay if I go first? Can you collect your thoughts while I give you mine?

ABIGAIL. Yes. I'll be ready by the time you're done, Rachel.

BETHANY. Then, let's get started. As moderator, well, I ask that you be adults and well, just speak...with respect... and, um...clarity. After you each say your piece... *(Smiles.)* while keeping your peace...then you can ask each other questions...calmly.

RACHEL. *(Snapping.)* Got it! I'm ready. Can we just do this?

BETHANY. *(Claps back.)* You wanted me to moderate. I'm just trying to explain the rules, Rachel. Do not bite my head off!

RACHEL. Sorry, didn't mean to snap. *(Sweetly.)* I got it. Thank you, Bethany.

BETHANY. You're welcome. And please let each other finish. No interruptions.

RACHEL. Got it.

ABIGAIL. Me too. I got it, too.

BETHANY. Alright, then. Rachel, please tell Abigail all you need to say.

RACHEL. You took his life. And you ruined mine. You destroyed your own life and what you did can never be undone. *(Starts to break, deep breath, gathers strength.)* I have searched my soul. I have prayed...even fasted. I. Have. Tried. Tried to forgive you. You were...are... my sister. We were so close. Once. Beth, I love you, you know that...but it was different with me and Abigail. She was my first sister and when Mama brought you home, she told me that you were all mine. My very own live doll baby. I abandoned all my other dolls because I had my own live doll baby. Abby. When Daddy left, we got even closer...couldn't be separated. We clung to each other so hard. You were the harmony to my melody. I know that sounds corny and cliché, but it's true. Oh, we fought. Nobody fought harder or louder than you. Nobody got madder. But we always made up. But this... how –? How? I miss my doll baby sister, but I just don't think we can ever – *(Tears.)* You took so much from me that day. You took him. And you. You took *you.* And when I see him, feed him, love on him...I'm reminded of what you did and all you took...and forgiveness I have found is...is just not possible. *(Pause.)* I guess... I'm done. That's all. For now. I'm done.

BETHANY. That was real good, Rachel. I'm proud of you. Direct and honest. Abigail, did you hear what Rachel had to say?

     *(**ABIGAIL** nods.)*

And are you ready? Did you collect your own thoughts?

ABIGAIL. I think so. *(Deep, nervous breath.)* I'll start with...I'm very sorry. I'm not sure I've ever... *(Laughs nervously.)* I feel like...this is one of those trials on TV where the killer apologizes to the family before the sentencing.

(Silence.) I understand your anger, Rachel, that you can't forgive me. Because I can't forgive you either –

RACHEL. You can't forgive me –?

BETHANY. Please, no. Save it.

RACHEL. *(Frustrated.)* Okay!

ABIGAIL. No, I can't. What I did was so wrong, but at least I have been able to see that. Accountability. There is none...was none...not one iota of accountability on your end.

> *(She gets up and gets Rachel's white Bible where it sits by her computer. She thumbs through as she returns to her seat.)*

Mama used to read us this scripture. James 2:10...that Mama made us memorize...

> *(She hands the Bible to* **RACHEL** *as she recites.)*

"For whosoever shall keep the whole law, and yet offend in one point, he is guilty of all." That means... we were taught by Mama, by the church, that – all sins are equal. So my sins are not bigger than yours, Rachel. That's what we were taught. And your sins created the...this mess that caused mine. Lying. Betraying. Stealing. *(Hard, slow, deliberate.)* You stole my fiancé. You took him. You....Jude...started up behind my back and never once told me. Just deceived! Jude was the love of my life first, and you had to take him! Had to have him. And this wasn't a lavender bow, Rachel. I told you how much... *(Emotion starts pouring now.)* how much I loved him. We talked about it. You acted like you were so happy for us. Like sisters should be. You agreed to be my maid of honor. Agreed to be my maid of honor then...YOU TOOK JUDE, just took him. And he was not yours to take!! So where is my apology? Huh? Sorry, Beth...I'll ask that later. But I'm not expecting an answer because you have never,

ever in your life been capable of being wrong! I fought so hard because I had to! You were the prettiest, the oldest. Bethany was the baby, the best singer...with that body. I was...just...stuck...stuck in the middle. And what was mine...what I finally had that was just mine – you stole, just took! What kind of person...what kind of Christian...what kind of sister does that? *(Pause.)* So...I can't forgive you either, Rachel. And I certainly cannot forgive myself. *(Pause, breaks.)* But I would like to be your doll baby again. Your sister. But...these... permanent circumstances that we both caused...no sin is greater...prevents that...and I simply do not know how! And for that, I'm most sorry of all.

> *(RACHEL leaps up, rushes out the front door, and screams a gut-wrenching, almost animalistic cry of pain, anger, grief, and regret. ABIGAIL and BETHANY stare after her in silence, stunned. Then it's over. She walks back in the door, tears running down her face.)*

RACHEL. This horror. The deed. Deeds. You are right. They cannot be undone. This cannot be fixed. Ever. All these years I thought...and I thought that your act, that horrible rage-induced act, negated what I did to you. But that...that is not the case. So, I'm sorry. *(Then the floodgates open.)* And if you don't think I'm capable... I'm here to tell you right now that... *(Deep sigh.)* I was wrong! *(Long pause.)* But this life...these acts...these circumstances...have destroyed us!

> *(Blackout.)*

Scene Four

(Day five.)

(In darkness, we hear the end of a gospel song from a male trio and applause.*)

MALE VOICE. Thank you! And Ditty, thank you so very much for including me and my brothers in your special night. Your music got me through some dark times. So, y'all...without further ado, please make welcome to the stage the woman of the hour, the national treasure we are all celebrating here tonight. Ditty Blaylock!

> *(Audience applause as a spotlight hits a microphone, perhaps on the landing or somewhere in the theatre or stage that can serve as the stage for Ditty's special.* **DITTY,** *in a beautiful dress, enters and walks to the microphone.)*

DITTY. Oh, you beautiful people. I'm at a loss for words. A pure loss for words. And ask anybody who knows me well, that unto itself is a slight miracle! This night has meant so much. So very, very much. I truly feel that I could die and go to heaven now. How in the world can anything top this? Oh wait, wait...maybe something can. See, there is one final act. One final number. A surprise. Once upon a time, there were three little girls who would sing their hearts out for Jesus. Little superstars for Jesus. There was Rachel, there was Abigail and there was Bethany. And tonight, for the first time in almost twenty-five years, they have reunited. Not just in the flesh, but – *(Chokes up.)* as

---

*A license to produce *This Side of Crazy* does not include a performance license for any third-party or copyrighted music. Licensees should create an original composition or use music in the public domain. For further information, please see Music and Third-Party Materials Use Note on page iii.

sisters who have come together in the love that they have for one another...and for their mama. Ladies and gentlemen, it is my extreme pleasure to give you my precious, precious, precious daughters, the loves of my life – The Blaylock Sisters!

*(Applause as **RACHEL**, **ABIGAIL**, and **BETHANY** enter. **DITTY** kisses each one as they take the microphone.)*

[MUSIC CUE: "CITY OF GOLD" TRACK]

(The sisters sing in perfect three-part harmony.)

RACHEL, ABIGAIL & BETHANY.
THERE'S A CITY THAT LOOKS O'ER THE VALLEY OF DEATH.
AND ITS GLORY HAS NEVER BEEN TOLD.
WHERE THE LAMB IS THE LIGHT, IN THE MIDST OF THE NIGHT,
IN THAT BEAUTIFUL CITY OF GOLD.

BETHANY.
WHERE THE SUN.

RACHEL & ABIGAIL.
WHERE THE SUN.

BETHANY.
NEVER SETS.

RACHEL & ABIGAIL.
NEVER SETS.

BETHANY.
AND THE LEAVES.

RACHEL & ABIGAIL.
AND THE LEAVES.

BETHANY.
NEVER FADE.

RACHEL & ABIGAIL.
> NEVER FADE.

RACHEL, ABIGAIL & BETHANY.
> WHERE THE RIGHTEOUS FOREVER WILL SHINE LIKE THE
> STARS,
> IN THAT BEAUTIFUL CITY OF GOLD.

RACHEL.
> THERE WILL BE NO MORE SORROW, PAIN, SICKNESS OR
> DEATH.

BETHANY.
> AND THE SAINTS THERE WILL NEVER GROWN OLD.

ABIGAIL.
> HOW I LONG FOR THAT CITY, WHERE THERE NEVER
> COMES A NIGHT.

RACHEL, ABIGAIL & BETHANY.
> IN THAT BEAUTIFUL CITY OF GOLD.

BETHANY.
> WHERE THE SUN.

RACHEL & ABIGAIL.
> WHERE THE SUN.

BETHANY.
> NEVER SETS.

RACHEL & ABIGAIL.
> NEVER SETS.

BETHANY.
> AND THE LEAVES.

RACHEL & ABIGAIL.
> AND THE LEAVES.

BETHANY.
> NEVER FADE.

RACHEL & ABIGAIL.
NEVER FADE.

RACHEL, ABIGAIL & BETHANY.
WHERE THE RIGHTEOUS FOREVER WILL SHINE LIKE THE
STARS,
IN THAT BEAUTIFUL CITY OF GOLD.

We love you, Mama!

(Spotlight out on key change. **BETHANY,**
RACHEL, *and* **ABIGAIL** *exit as the song*
transitions into:)

(Family room. Lights up on **DITTY,** *sitting in*
her chair in one of her muumuus, watching
her special on TV, gun in her lap covered by
a letter and will. She smiles and occasionally
wipes away tears.)

BETHANY. *(On TV.)*
WHERE. THE. SUN.

RACHEL & ABIGAIL. *(On TV.)*
WHERE THE SUN.

BETHANY. *(On TV.)*
NEVER SETS.

RACHEL & ABIGAIL. *(On TV.)*
NEVER SETS.

BETHANY. *(On TV.)*
AND THE LEAVES.

RACHEL & ABIGAIL. *(On TV.)*
AND THE LEAVES.

BETHANY. *(On TV.)*
NEVER FADE.

RACHEL, ABIGAIL & BETHANY. *(On TV.)*
> WHERE THE RIGHTEOUS FOREVER WILL SHINE LIKE THE
> STARS,
> IN THAT BEAUTIFUL CITY OF GOLD.

BETHANY. *(On TV.)*
> AND THE LEAVES.

RACHEL & ABIGAIL. *(On TV.)*
> AND THE LEAVES.

BETHANY. *(On TV.)*
> NEVER FADE.

RACHEL, ABIGAIL & BETHANY. *(On TV.)*
> WHERE THE RIGHTEOUS FOREVER WILL SHINE LIKE THE
> STARS, IN THAT BEAUTIFUL CITY OF GOLD.
> IN THAT BEAUTIFUL CITY OF GOLD.

> *(The song ends to thunderous applause.* **DITTY**
> *sighs, turns off the TV, then walks over to the
> gun drawer, opens it, and places the will and
> letter in it. She closes the drawer, then walks
> out the front door with the gun.)*

> *(Count five. Offstage. Gunshot.)*

> *(Blackout.)*

Scene Five

(Day six. A few days after the gunshot.)

*(Family room. Lights up as **BETHANY** enters, wearing black with yellow accessories, followed by **RACHEL** wearing black with pink accessories, and **ABIGAIL** wearing black with lavender accessories. **RACHEL** carries a potted plant, drops her purse by the door, then on the table, then heads up the stairs to the porch.)*

BETHANY. That was a lot. Long. Reminded me of why I haven't been in church in...well, forever. Hopefully, I'll die first so I don't have to go to your funerals!

> *(**BETHANY** drops her purse on the table, kicks off her shoes, sits at the table, and props her feet up on a chair.)*

> *(Porch. **RACHEL** places the plant on the porch.)*

ABIGAIL. But it was nice. Mama would have loved that people were spilling out of the church into the yard and all the way down the street.

BETHANY. One couple told me they flew in from Australia.

> *(**RACHEL** exits the porch and crosses the hallway to the bedroom.)*

RACHEL. *(Calling down the stairs.)* But...it was long.

> *(Bedroom. **RACHEL** enters and checks on Jude, lost in thought for a long moment.)*

ABIGAIL. *(Yelling so **RACHEL** can hear.)* And she would have loved that so many sang her songs. Sandi Patty especially. She said to me...the nicest thing to me privately. And I told her Mama said she was her favorite singer and that Mama said just before the special that when she imagines angels singing, it's a choir of Sandi Pattys.

(RACHEL closes the bedroom door, comes back down the stairs.)

RACHEL. That would be too much soprano.

(BETHANY and ABIGAIL laugh.)

BETHANY. Way too much. I need to go for a run. I'm starving, but I need to run before I eat. I'm going to go change –

RACHEL. Well, before you do...no go...go change, but I need to tell you both...well some things...and show you something before you run –

(RACHEL picks up and hands BETHANY her shoes and purse.)

BETHANY. I'll be fast.

(BETHANY exits up the stairs and through the landing door to the other part of the house.)

RACHEL. What did Sandi Patty say...to you...privately?

ABIGAIL. That Mama touched more lives than any person she could think of...with her music. Her songs –

RACHEL. Yeah, I guess she did. You don't think anybody suspected do you?

ABIGAIL. I don't think so.

RACHEL. Cost me a grand in cash to pay off the coroner. Worth every penny. I couldn't have taken the humiliation...the judgment...the questions. The press. She had a heart attack. Simple. Clean. *(Distant.)* Maybe I am just like Mama. Two peas in a pod.

(*A moment of awkward silence, then* **RACHEL** *goes to the gun drawer and pulls out a will, an envelope of Ditty's stationary, a can of Vienna sausages, and one other piece of paper. She heads back to the table.*)

RACHEL. (*Calling.*) Bethany –?! You coming?!

(**BETHANY** *reappears wearing her running clothes as* **RACHEL** *pulls a note out of Ditty's stationary.*)

BETHANY. Is that a can of Vienna sausages? Oh my God, it is!

Yes. Sit. Please.

(**BETHANY** *sits and smiles weakly at* **ABIGAIL**, *who also sits.* **RACHEL** *takes the can of Vienna sausages, exits to the kitchen.*)

BETHANY. (*Calling.*) What are you doing, Rachel?

RACHEL. (*Offstage.*) You'll see.

(*She returns and puts the now-open can down on the table.*)

Okay, well, I'm the executor of... And yes, Mama left us a will and... (*Laughs.*) a can of Vienna sausages. (*Shows them the outside of the envelope.*) Says: "To My Little Superstars For Jesus. Eat one sausage, then read my note and my will, then eat your other sausage." So... okay, two each just like when we were little. Let's all eat one and then I'll read Mama's note.

(**RACHEL** *takes a sausage and passes the can to* **ABIGAIL**, *who takes one and passes the can to* **BETHANY**, *who takes one. They all eat their sausages.*)

BETHANY. This is so weird.

(They each finish a sausage.)

Just read it, Rachel. I'm ready.

(BETHANY takes ABIGAIL's hand.)

RACHEL. Okay. *(Picks up the note, reads.)* "My precious little superstars for Jesus. I'm sorry I had to leave, but it was simply time. This old show pony was done. After that beautiful television tribute for me, I just didn't have anything else to offer this world...or you. My darlings, I did not want to return to unhappy days. I simply could not bear it. And quite frankly, I could offer you a whole lot more after my exit. Unlike in life, I will not drone on, so I leave you with this. Reclaim the love you once had for each other, because I promise, it is still there! Find forgiveness for each other – and for me. The key to forgiveness is the good memories. Reclaim those good memories, suppress all the bad ones, and go make more good ones. Rachel, Abigail, Bethany, I love you with all my heart and to the depths of my very soul. And always remember, you let your mama die happy."

(Silence.)

She left us very well off. And Abigail...Abby...I had this drawn up.

(RACHEL hands ABIGAIL the piece of paper. ABIGAIL reads it, looks up. BETHANY gives ABIGAIL's hand a supportive squeeze, then takes the will and starts looking through it.)

ABIGAIL. Does this mean –?

RACHEL. You're free...if you want to be. Nobody is your legal guardian except you now. I know. It's a lot...a lot to process.

BETHANY. *(Re: the will.)* Whoa –

RACHEL. Yes, she had lots in the bank. Plus, the thousands of cash she has hoarded all over the house...and we get her royalties and publishing for the rest of our lives. And both of you have your share of the Blaylock Sisters' royalties in a trust she was...well, keeping for...well, *from* you.

BETHANY. *(This sinks in.)* You mean...I've been...barely surviving and she...you knew?! Rachel, you knew she was doing this to me and –

RACHEL. Stop! Listen to me! I made mistakes. *(To* **ABIGAIL.***)* So many. But Mama...she was just such a force and...I was wrong, Beth. So wrong. And I'm sorry. But she no longer controls you. Not anymore! Nor you, Abigail. *(Realizing.)* Or me. Let's let that sink in. Please, let's just let that sink in.

> *(They all do.)*

BETHANY. Oh my God! *(Emotional.)* I can stop...I can stop this desperate need to survive.

> *(***RACHEL*** puts her arms around* **BETHANY,** *then tentatively around* **ABIGAIL.***)*

RACHEL. Okay, let's eat our other Vienna sausage.

> *(***BETHANY*** grabs her second one and passes the can to* **RACHEL,** *who takes hers, then passes the can to* **ABIGAIL,** *who takes the last one. They eat simultaneously.* **ABIGAIL** *suddenly starts giggling.)*

ABIGAIL. I just had a good memory. In the back seat –

BETHANY. Of that car Uncle Junior gave us!

> *(They all laugh, remembering.)*

RACHEL. When we were on that car church tour. *(Realizes.)* Oh! Mama knew! She knew we'd find a good memory.

BETHANY. In a Vienna sausage!

RACHEL. Maybe she does still control us.

ABIGAIL. I need a cigarette.

> (**ABIGAIL** *takes the release form and heads up the stairs.* **RACHEL** *stares at her as she exits onto the porch.*)

BETHANY. Oh, my God, this day.

> (**RACHEL** *heads up the stairs as* **BETHANY** *heads to the front door.*)

> (*Music cue, almost distant, of the Blaylock Sisters, as children, singing: "Farther along we'll know all about it, Farther along we'll understand why."* Music continues to the end of the play.*)

> (**BETHANY** *pauses by the door, stares at a picture of* **DITTY**, *then suddenly collapses into a heap of emotion. Lights fade slowly on* **BETHANY** *as she recovers, the crying transitioning into full laugher as she runs out the front door.*)

> (*Landing.* **RACHEL** *starts to enter Jude's bedroom but pauses, turns, and stares at* **ABIGAIL** *for a moment on the porch as she sits in the rocker, lighting a cigarette and reading the paper Rachel gave her.* **RACHEL** *then turns and enters the bedroom. She stares at Jude. She walks over to the bed, removes his feeding and hydration tubes, then pushes the stand into a corner.*)

---

*A license to produce *This Side of Crazy* does not include a performance license for any third-party or copyrighted recordings. Licensees must create their own, using public domain music.

RACHEL. *(Softly.)* It's time. Time to...move on.

(Tears fill her eyes as she walks back to the bed and climbs in beside Jude as lights fade in the bedroom.)

(Porch. ABIGAIL smokes and rocks. She looks out at the sunset as lights slowly begin to fade.)

(Blackout.)

(Only the light of ABIGAIL's cigarette is left burning on the porch as the girls finish the song: "We'll understand it all by and by." Cigarette out.)

End of Play

PROPERTY PLOT

Act One Presets

Family Room: remote control, Ditty's coffee mug, pistol and ammo, Rachel's laptop, Rachel's white Bible, tissues, video tapes, framed photo of younger girls, stationary and pen, telephone, tripod with iPhone (hidden from view), Rachel's purse, Bethany's pills

Bedroom: medical supplies on nightstand, IV stand, feeding bags, picture of Jude on wall

Porch: terracotta pot/saucer, broom, watering can

Landing: sheets and blanket in dresser

Offstage: cup of coffee, pre-addressed envelopes, Bethany's suitcase and purse, unsigned check, envelope of cash, pair of full Dollar-Store grocery bags (one containing a can of Cook's Chili, can of Diet Coke, Abigail's suitcase, Abigail's cigarettes and lighter)

Act Two Presets

Family Room: sheet music on piano, wad of cash (hidden in drawer), place setting for four taken from credenza (napkins, napkin rings, bowls, spoons, glasses), bread box with partial loaf of white bread inside, pad of paper and pen, Vienna sausages, Abigail's release form (hidden in drawer), framed photo of Ditty

Offstage: dish towel, soup tureen of pre-heated chili, pitcher of iced tea, standing microphone, Ditty's parting letter and will, funeral plant

COSTUME PLOT

DITTY

Act One, Scene One: teal blouse (worn all of Act One), orange & teal paisley muumuu #1, orange & teal paisley turban #1, beige flats, orange necklace and earrings #1, watch and rings (worn throughout)

Act One, Scene Two: peach & turquoise floral muumuu #2, peach & turquoise turban #2 with rhinestone flower brooch, same flats

Act One, Scene Three: brown wig, red & blue floral pantsuit #1 with rhinestone rose brooch, silver sandals, silver crucifix necklace and earrings #2, beige & gold leopard purse

Act One, Scene Four: same

Act Two, Scene One: same wig and accessories, blue animal print pantsuit #2

Act Two, Scene Two: same

Act Two, Scene Three: same

Act Two, Scene Four: Show: two-piece flowing off-white blouse and palazzo pants constructed from satin/lace/chiffon and bejeweled with crystals and rhinestones, "diamond" and "white gold" rings, bracelets and drop earrings, silver lame' bib necklace, silver low-heeled sandals, satin & rhinestone headband over wig for a halo effect, cream-colored & lace-edged handkerchief

Transition to a few days after the special: same accessories worn throughout play except for tribute, green floral-print muumuu #3, green turban #3

NOTE: Ditty's costume plot from NCTC San Francisco premiere production except for Ditty's Tribute costume. That costume was from the LA production as that scene was changed from V.O. to live. Turbans were not worn by Ditty in the LA production. Instead, gray hair at home and an eventful red wig when Ditty dressed to go out.

RACHEL

Act One, Scene One: pink bra & panties, light pink short-sleeve button-down blouse #1, dark-pink floral skirt #1, pink sling-back kitten heels #1, pearl crucifix necklace & earrings #1 and rhinestone bracelet (worn entire act), wedding ring (worn entire show)

Act One, Scene Two: pink pleated blouse #2, gray slacks, mauve kitten heels #2

Act One, Scene Three: same blouse and shoes, pink bouclé skirt #2, pink bouclé jacket, magenta purse

Act One, Scene Four: same

Act Two, Scene One: dusty pink floral blouse #3 and dusty pink pleated skirt #3, burgundy ballet flats

Act Two, Scene Two: same

Act Two, Scene Three: same

Act Two, Scene Four: pink dress #1, pink sling-back heels from Act One, Scene One

Act Two, Scene Five: black & pink dress #2, black heels #3

BETHANY

Act One, Scene Two: white push-up bra with inserts (worn entire show), zip jeans #1, yellow strawberries tank-top #1, black fringe cowboy boots #1, black grommet belt #1, yellow bracelet and dangly necklace & earrings (worn until Act One, Scene Four), rings (worn entire show)

Act One, Scene Three: same boots and jeans, yellow & white string tank-top #2, black & brown purse

Act One, Scene Four: gray mesh yoga pants, tight gold tank-top #3, aqua sneakers

Act Two, Scene One: sequined jeans #2, yellow snaps t-shirt #1, black & brown cowboy boots #2

Act Two, Scene Two: same

Act Two, Scene Three: same

Act Two, Scene Four: yellow dress, cream heels

Act Two, Scene Five: black pinstripe slacks, mustard ruffle blouse, black pinstripe jacket, black ankle boots #2, quick change into Act One, Scene Four yoga pants, gold v-neck t-shirt #2, Act One, Scene Four sneakers

ABIGAIL

Act One, Scene Three: camisole (worn entire show), floral-print dress #1, taupe flats #1

Act One, Scene Four: worn lavender robe, plaid pajama pants #1, same flats

Act Two, Scene One: violet tunic blouse, brown pants #2, Act One, Scene Four robe (removed), flats

Act Two, Scene Two: same

Act Two, Scene Three: same

Act Two, Scene Four: lavender plaid dress #2, beige heels

Act Two, Scene Five: black dress #3, black flats #2

City of Gold

Arranged by Amy Meyers

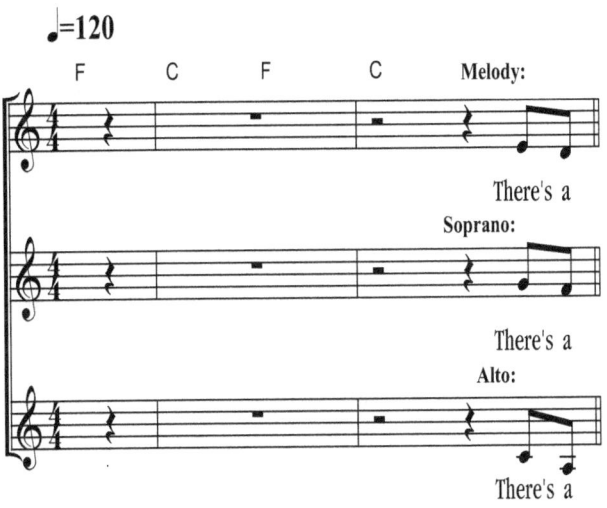

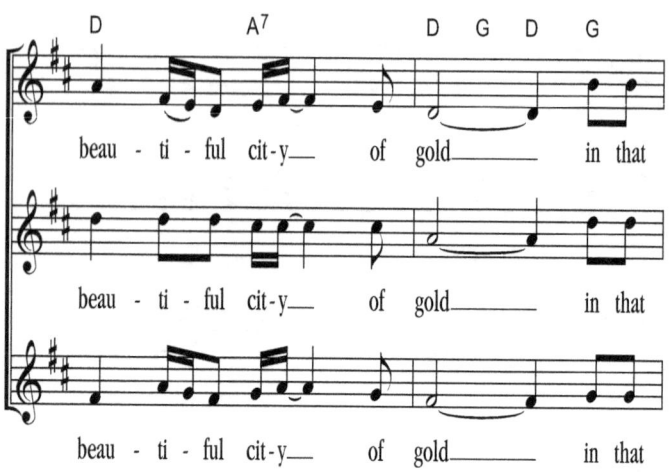

beau - ti - ful cit-y— of gold———— in that

beau - ti - ful cit-y— of gold———— in that

beau - ti - ful cit-y— of gold———— in that

rit.

beau - ti - ful cit-y— of gold——————

beau - ti - ful cit-y— of gold——————

beau - ti - ful cit-y— of gold——————

www.ingramcontent.com/pod-product-compliance
Lightning Source LLC
Chambersburg PA
CBHW071929130726
47909CB00014B/2740